T0103459

CRIMSON TIES

CRIMSON
TIES

DONNA IRVING

PARTRIDGE

Copyright © 2017 by Donna Irving.

Library of Congress Control Number:		2016944347
ISBN:	Hardcover	978-1-4828-6665-0
	Softcover	978-1-4828-6664-3
	eBook	978-1-4828-6666-7

All rights reserved. No part of this book may be used or reproduced by any means, graphic, electronic, or mechanical, including photocopying, recording, taping or by any information storage retrieval system without the written permission of the author except in the case of brief quotations embodied in critical articles and reviews.

Because of the dynamic nature of the Internet, any web addresses or links contained in this book may have changed since publication and may no longer be valid. The views expressed in this work are solely those of the author and do not necessarily reflect the views of the publisher, and the publisher hereby disclaims any responsibility for them.

Print information available on the last page.

To order additional copies of this book, contact
Toll Free 800 101 2657 (Singapore)
Toll Free 1 800 81 7340 (Malaysia)
orders.singapore@partridgepublishing.com

www.partridgepublishing.com/singapore

Contents

PROLOGUE

THE ROOM WAS SILENT EXCEPT for the soft creaking of the pen being manoeuvred across paper. A lone woman sat behind a mahogany desk, focusing intensely on what she was writing. The only light to assist her being that of a single candle sitting by her hand. The lighting was poor but with her eyesight, it was really only an accessory.

"Done," she huffed, letting out a puff of air as she reclined in the black leather chair.

A knock came on the door, resounding in the study made of stone. The woman looked up, her chocolate orbs gazing at the arched, wooden door.

"Mary?" A woman called through the door.

Recognising the voice, Mary responded. "Come in, Sera."

The door opened and Sera entered, her delicate wings of green and blue fluttering behind her.

"The others sent me to retrieve you," she explained. "Dinner is ready."

Mary nodded, smiling. "Thanks. I'll be down in a sec, okay?"

She looked at all the paper strewn about on the desk curiously. "What are you up to?"

Mary hesitated for a moment before giving in. "I'm just retelling our story."

Sera frowned in confusion. "What do you mean?"

"Well, my dad had a diary so I thought maybe I should start one too."

"That's actually a good idea," Sera stated.

"Don't sound so surprised, Sera," Mary laughed. "I can have good ideas when I want to."

Sera turned bright red. "No! That isn't what I meant!" She rushed.

Mary laughed again. "I'm just teasing, Sera."

Her head turned and her gaze was drawn out the window where the sounds of the city could still be heard.

"How are you doing?" Sera finally spoke up after several minutes of silence.

"Not too good," Mary answered. "I'm under so much stress right now and with Aimee having taken off like that..."

"She'll be back," Sera encouraged. "She just needs time to cool off."

"Yeah, maybe."

"Come on. Let's go down for dinner," Sera stated. "You've been locked away in here for a few days now."

"You know why."

"I do and I'm glad you're taking your responsibilities seriously," she complimented, tidying up the mess of papers upon the desk. "But you need to take care of yourself. You're going to run yourself into the ground."

Mary didn't answer but made to grab the pen when Sera picked it up instead.

"Sera..."

Sera shook her head. "No. You need to eat."

Mary let out an exaggerated sigh but rose from her chair.

"Alright, you win."

Sera watched as the dhampir left the study, leaving the door open for her. Putting the pen back down, the fairy's eyes were drawn to Mary's latest writings.

1

THE FAMILY

THE TARGET BUILDING WAS AN abandoned warehouse. The walls were faded, dank and dirty with neglect, having been abandoned for over twenty years now.

"Mary, how's your side?" Chelsea's voice sounded in my head.

She was the last one I met out of my friends, but the oldest at twenty-five. Her parents were actually the ones to Turn her.

To be Turned is to be changed by a vampire. This happens when a vampire drains its victim of blood and feeds them their own. Not many have the control to do this, as the taste of blood can easily send a vampire into a frenzy and most just suck their prey dry.

There are also the True Born, born vampires. They can only belong to one of the six ancient families that reside in Tavina, the world where all supernatural beings originate. Only they have the ability to reproduce. They age at the same rate as a human and only stop once they reach their prime.

Draconis and Vipera are two powerful kingdoms that rule over most of Tavina. They're made up of three ancient vampire clans -with one of them ruling over the other two- and three powerful alliances.

"Mary, are you okay?" Tori asked.

Her name was actually Victoria but everyone calls her Tori. She's also a Turned. She *was* a vampire hunter last year until I had Chelsea change her but that's a story for another time.

"I'm fine," I replied. *"Sorry, I was thinking."*

"You had me worried there for a second," Bethany huffed.

Bethany is an air elemental, a human with the ability to manipulate wind. There are those with the ability to control one of the four elements but most of them, if not all, stay in Tavina near their creators.

Suddenly, I saw something shift in my peripheral vision.

"I've got movement," I mentally stated as I drew my pistols.

Some vampires -the stronger ones at least- can move faster then a flying bullet so guns would be useless against them. The weaker ones -normally the newborns- haven't developed enough as a vampire to use their abilities to their fullest and thus cannot dodge fast enough. Luckily, I've been trained in swords and daggers in case they do dodge.

Some vampires also develop a special ability, depending on who their Turner is or how strong they are. It's actually thanks to Chelsea who shares a drop of blood with us all once a week to keep up this mental connection that we have since she herself holds the power of telepathy. A drop of her blood and we're able to speak telepathically to one another.

The sound of gunshots resonated through the empty warehouse and I turned my head towards the sound.

"Who was that?" Tori asked.

"If that wasn't you, there's more than one here. Keep an eye out for more and watch your back," I ordered. *"Check on Chelsea and back her up. I want to kill these bastards as soon as possible."*

I knew it wasn't Chelsea because she doesn't use guns. Swords are her specialty. She'd have you diced up before you knew it thanks to her twin bayonets that she keeps on her almost all of the time. You can never guess how many blades she hides.

Tori was known as the Weapon Mistress due to her mastery of every weapon. She could tell you what weapon killed who from wherever and whenever just from looking at a wound. Not to mention, she could make a weapon out of anything and think of many different ways to kill you with it.

I was brought out of my thoughts when something launched itself out of the shadows towards me. It landed a kick to my side and I went face first into the wall beside me. I fell to the ground with a groan, taking a moment to recover.

There was a figure to my right that caught my eye. Turning, I found the corpse of a little girl. She had to have been no older than nine years old.

Anger consumed me. I stood to face my attacker but my guns lay a couple meters away from me where the surprise attack had loosened my grip. He was an older man, around forty years of age with skin almost aglow, a known phenomenon that happens when a vampire has just fed on fresh blood. It rejuvenates their dead cells, making them seem ethereal.

He threw himself at me again but this time, I was ready. Before he reached me, I grabbed his outstretched arm and spun, slamming him into the wall with as much force as I could. He hit the wall face-first, like I had just moments before. To my satisfaction, I heard his nose crack. I wasn't fooled though. It takes more than a face full of stone to kill a bloodsucker.

I grabbed the back of his neck and threw him down to the ground, straddling him in the blink of an eye. His cheekbone was shattered and his face dinted in but I'd seen it all before. I didn't think twice about pounding my fists into his face repeatedly.

Only a few minutes later did I stop, panting from adrenaline and anger. I glared down at his bloodied face. Deciding I should end it, I stabbed my right hand into his chest, straight through his ribs for my signature ending. He screamed and thrashed about but I was much stronger. I didn't train day in, day out for nothing.

I gripped his heart and tore it from his body, watching as his crimson eyes faded to blue, his natural colour and hollowed of the life that once filled them. His face remained contorted in silent scream of agony.

"I hope that hurt."

I stayed there for a second before slowly standing. My hands were tainted red with blood that had also splattered my clothes. I dropped the heart and wiped my hands on my jeans (they were going into the wash anyway) before picking up my guns and walking to the smaller corpse.

I knelt down and picked up the little girls' body after holstering my guns. She was so tiny. She had long, beautiful golden hair. She would have been a gorgeous little girl and a joy to watch running around but her body was cooling rapidly and it cut me deeply knowing that I could have saved her if I had been faster.

Even though I've been surrounded by death since the tender age of five, it doesn't mean I'm numb to it.

"I can't sense anyone else here. I think there were only two," Chelsea said. *"The woman we fought was pretty weak. How are things on your end, Mary?"*

"The target's been eliminated."

"Was there a death?" Tori asked.

I sighed. *"Yeah. You guys head home. I'll give Brenton a call. He can take the body."*

I didn't want to spend more time here then I had to.

"Will you be alright?" Bethany asked.

"Yeah. I'll see you back at home," I replied before I headed out of the dreary warehouse.

I pulled my phone and dialled '2' where Brent's number came up and began to ring.

Brent Xander is a sergeant of the Police Force for the city. He has a lot of experience since his father is the Chief of Police. Brenton's also my informant and provides us with our missions. That's what my friends and I do. We hunt those that prey on the weak. We defend those who can't defend themselves but if we can't, we hunt down the ones responsible.

"What've you got for me?"

"There were two vampires in the building, not one," I stated.

"You alright?"

"Aw, you do care," I cooed and he scoffed. *"Yeah, we're fine. We took care of both."*

"I'll look into my sources. Sorry about that," he apologised. *"I'll send a clean up team."*

"Okay, but we have a corpse."

There was a pause. *"How old?"*

"Nine."

"Shit," he cursed. *"Alright, I'll be there soon."*

We met a few years ago, during one of my missions. He had heard about me and wanted to meet me in person. First, we talked business, about how he would supply me with hunts so I could help him keep the city safe. Then, it went from partners to friends.

About fifteen minutes later, a van pulled up. Several people climbed out, Brenton being one of them. He walked to me as a few of his men entered the building.

"She's a gorgeous little girl," Brenton said softly.

I nodded. "She was."

He frowned before one of his men took her from me. We both watched as they placed her in a body bag and then into the white van, alongside her murderer. Well, what was left of him.

"Are you alright?" He asked, turning back to me.

I met his eyes before adverting them.

"I'm good. He wasn't too strong-"

"You know what I mean, Mary."

I sighed and turned away. "Yeah, I'm pretty cut up over it but it happens."

"I know. I just want to make sure you'll be okay," he spoke blandly, but I knew it was his way of dealing with emotional situations.

"I'll be fine. I just want to go home and take a nice bath."

He nodded. "Alright then, go. Get a good rest and I'll call you tomorrow to see how you're doing," he promised.

I nodded and headed home by foot since the girls and I only lived

My name is Mary Hazel, though that's not my true name. Every noble Ascuns (supernatural being) is given a Vala; a true name. They do this to hide any titles from possible enemies and to fit into today's society. It's what killed my parents.

My parents were murdered by a large gang of vampires looking for my father specifically. I remember nothing of our attackers, only that they all had a tattoo of a snake on their wrists.

It's looked down upon in the vampire race for a True Born vampire such as my Dad to love a human like my Mom. Dhampirs though, they're absolutely despised amongst the vampire kind. To them, I am some disgusting act of shame committed by my parents. But they loved each other and they loved me. That's all I care about.

When I was five, we were attacked by a small army of vampires. Dad fought to protect both my Mom and I. He fought long and hard, killing many while in what has now been explained to me as a vampiric rage called Hysteria. It's something only a few vampires can activate when they are pushed to their limit.

But he was overwhelmed and both my Mom and I had to witness my Dad's defeat, though he took most of them with him. Those that survived relished in his death. I had to watch my Dad being murdered by his own kind, simply because he fell in love with a human.

My father loved me. Even though I had been only young, I know he did. He had told me what he was and that what he did was looked down upon and despite having lost his family in Tavina, he didn't regret a thing because he had Mom and I. I was his little angel and he didn't see me as a disgrace but as the result of his love for Mom. He told me they were *blessed* to have me and wouldn't trade me for the world. I was his princess and Mom was his queen.

When we cried out for him, the rest of the vampires turned to us. Mom grabbed me and made a run for it but someone grabbed her hair and pulled her back. She pushed me away from her and I rolled on the ground. I was forced to watch as the vampires violated her brutally before killing her. She, too, had been torn from me. I experienced Hysteria myself as my anger and will to survive kicked into overdrive and somehow managed to kill those that remained. I don't remember that fight but I have scars from it, all over my arms.

Even though it was vampires that had ruined my life, they are a part of who I am. I accepted my Dad and inevitably, I accepted myself. I did not hate vampires because of those that took my parents, no. My Dad and my very existence taught me that not all vampires were cruel and prejudice. Dad showed me that he accepted this and that other vampires could too.

That's how I'm here today. My friends are a testimony to people like my Dad. They do not care what I am, whether I am True Born, Turned or Dhampir. To them, I am Mary and that's all they care about.

I touched the silver locket around my neck as I walked down the darkened street. My dad had given it to my mom. In the middle of the locket was a dark sapphire. Inside was a picture of Mom and Dad together in a loving embrace. He had mocha coloured skin, jet-black hair and brown eyes that flickered with emotion. He was tall and lean and had a small upside down triangular ruby on his forehead.

My mom was very beautiful. She had light brown hair and green eyes that held such love and compassion and never failed to show she loved my dad with a kiss. They were perfect for each other.

In the picture, they were both smiling. Mom was fat with pregnancy. Both of their hands were on her stomach where I had been, with Dad's hands on top of hers. The other picture was one of me at the age of three and was held between them. Even though I looked a lot like my dad, my personality mostly belonged to my mom, headstrong and emotional while my dad was calm and collected.

There were also two rings that had been found that belonged to my Dad. One was pure gold with rubies imbedded in the band and the other was a black dragon eating its own tail to form the ring. Those three things are all I have left of my parents and ever since they were returned to me, I've never taken them off. I was told that the rings were passed down in my dad's family and I have cherished them since.

Eventually, I stopped before another old warehouse. There was only once entrance of the two-story warehouse and that was into the bottom level where Tori, Chelsea and I stayed.

The windows were open to let in fresh air while its dark, otherwise they are closed with curtains to cover them up. On this level, there are three bedrooms, a training room, a bathroom and a toilet. We don't use this room much, only to sleep during the day. If we feel like staying up later or waking earlier, we have the training room to keep us occupied until we are ready to sleep. There is a ladder that we take up to the second floor, separated by an opening hatch to ensure no light comes in from the second level which holds many windows and openings.

While I can stand being in the sunlight, Chelsea and Tori cannot. The sun only hurts my eyes but it actually burns them so we need to take whatever precautions we can to protect them.

I climbed up to the second level to find Bethany and Sera watching cartoons in the lounge room. I looked around the area. Chelsea and Tori were at the dining table cleaning their weapons while Cassidy and Reign stood in the kitchen, arguing about what to make for dinner.

Seraphina -or Sera as we call her- is the first one of my friends that I met. We met when I was twelve. She comes from one of the ancient alliances I mentioned earlier. Her father is the current ruler of the Tima clan, making her a fairy and next in line for leadership, before her younger sister. She is a gentle soul, so caring and soft. She's almost the embodiment of innocence at its best.

Then we have the two angels, Cassidy and Reign. They met each other in an orphanage and it was hate at first sight. Somehow, that hatred then turned into best friendship. Cassidy has short, brown hair that make her sapphire blue eyes stand out.

Reign has curly light brown hair with wide, hazel green eyes that compliments her hair magnificently, giving her a native look.

While they have their similarities, they also have their differences. The best way to describe them would be the angel and demon on your shoulders. Cassidy is the optimism and hope for good while Reign is the brutal honesty that tempts your darker side.

There are many different supernatural beings in the world. Ascuns is what we call them. You read stories about there being only a few at a time, like vampires and werewolves or angels and demons. Truth is, there are fairies and fey, angels and demons, elementals, witches and necromancers, dragons and basilisks and vampires and werewolves. They all exist and have learnt over hundreds of years to co-exist with each other in the other world, Tavina.

"Welcome back," Cassidy greeted.

"Tori told us there was a death," Reign stated. "How old?"

I sighed. "Nine."

"Oh, no," Cassidy murmured.

"I just want to take a nice bath before going to bed," I murmured.

They were worried about me and I was grateful that I had such caring friends.

I went back down the ladder and then to the large bathroom. The room was practically made of cream coloured marble. Lights lit up around the mirror, brightening the room.

This whole place was done up by my late mentor, Amalia. She never told me her last name. She was the one that found me not long after my parents died. I was struggling to survive due to the fact that I didn't want to drink from a human. I couldn't find food since the vampires that killed my parents burnt down our house beforehand.

Amalia was an old vampire, passing through when she found me and brought me here. She became like a second mother to me as she taught me how to fight and survive. As I got older, she started to teach me how to use weapons and how to hunt. Being half-human, I could live on human food but it doesn't give me the strength I need.

When I was twelve, Amalia was killed by a vampire named Dorin. I lived here on my own, training so that one day I would find him and kill him.

I ran the bath and watched as it filled. Once it reached my desired height, I stripped down and stared at myself in the mirror. I inherited my mocha skin tone from my father, though I was lighter than him because of my mom's genes mixed in as well.

Staring at the mirror, my eyes instantly landed on the many scars on my left arm that I received that horrific night almost thirteen years ago. On the right of my left wrist was a bite scar from when I used my arm to stop a vampire from sinking his teeth into my neck. I had eight claw marks on the outside of my arm from when I was blocking myself from their attack. Two of the eight crossed over so you could tell they were from different times and not just one swipe. It kind of made my arm look like it had tiger stripes. Another scar ran under my upper arm, from my elbow to just short of my armpit where a vampire went for my heart and I dodged to the right and it got my arm. That last scar on my left arm was actually across my palm from where I stopped a sword from slicing me in half. That's only on my arm. On my back, I have a long scar running from my top left shoulder blade down to my lower right back. On my right shoulder blade were three clawing marks from a vampire who tried to grab me but I slipped away.

Because I was so young, I didn't know how to heal myself and scarred terribly. They will remain with me forever and only my friends know of my scars, hence why I constantly where a black elbow glove on my left arm or a long sleeve shirt. It also covered up my Dads' rings that I wore on my left ring finger and middle finger. They have not come off my finger since that night and I don't plan on it ever getting that pleasure. It's the same with the necklace that shone in the reflection brightly.

I have insecurities just like every other female teenager. The only difference is that I'm a hybrid and kill Ascuns nightly with my friends, but only the ones that kill for the fun of it. Ascuns are more than capable of not killing their prey so there is no excuse.

I fear, sometimes, that I'll one day slip. The memories, death and pain that surround me keep me in a constant limbo between sanity and madness. How I have lasted so long, I have no idea but I'm grateful I'm still in my right mind.

I climbed into the bath, soap suds clinging to my body before I fully relaxed in the steaming water. A sigh escapes me as I gave in to the feeling of warmth.

You'd think that after what happened to my parents that I'd hate to be around vampires like Chelsea or Tori but my Dad was living proof that there are vampires out there who could make a difference. My Dad loved my Mom and I, which means so can others and while I may not have the best life, I guess I could say I don't mind where I am. I have the best friends I could ever ask for and I have my reason for living. My name is Mary Catalina Hazel and this is only the beginning.

2

THE ROGUE

I JOLTED AWAKE WHEN I HEARD my mobile ringing. I rolled over and grabbed it off the mahogany bedside table, knocking over the lamp in my haste.

"Shit," I hissed before answering. "What?" I snapped.

I am definitely not a morning person as my friends found out the hard way. There was this one incident with Reign and Cassidy. Now no one even bothers me until after eleven.

"Hello to you, too," Brenton answered flatly.

I rolled my eyes before I realised he couldn't see the gesture. "I told you I'd call you in the morning. You know I don't get up until eleven. It's..." I paused as I regarded my internal clock. "Eight in the morning. Couldn't you have waited three hours?" I asked irately.

Being half vampire, you instinctively know where the sun is. Perhaps it was because some time long ago, vampires really *were* allergic to sunlight. Even though vampires these days can walk in broad daylight, it's basic instinct that tells us to stay away when all it does is hurt your eyes.

"Maybe I just wanted to hear your voice," he stated.

"Right."

Brenton's chuckle reached my ear.

I sighed. "Look, I'm fine, but I want to get back to sleep."

"Fine, I'll let you get back your coffin."

"I know you know that's a myth."

"Yes, but I also know you hate it when I make obscene movie references."

"Goodbye Brenton," I stressed out before hanging up and burying my head into my crimson duvet.

I hummed to myself softly and wiggled my toes as I drifted back to sleep.

~ X ~

I woke again a few hours later by a soft knock on the door. My eyes fluttered open and looked towards the door as Tori poked her head in.

"Lunch is ready downstairs," she spoke softly.

I nodded and got out of bed, letting my feet touch the fuzzy red carpet. I grabbed my phone and followed Tori out of my room and downstairs to the dining area. I sat at the head seat and looked at all the food made. Before me were fried eggs, bacon, scrambled eggs, toast, hash browns, spaghetti and a jug of blood from the blood packets Brenton kindly donates to us from the hospital. I hummed happily. We dug in, talking about what ever came to mind.

The loud tune of my phone reached my ears and I fished it out of my pocket.

"Talk to me."

"I've got your next hunt," Brenton's voice came through the receiver.

"I'm listening."

"Brunette women have been going missing from Blue Pulse, the new club that opened up a month ago," he debriefed. "Our recent witness said she was holding her friends hand when she disappeared."

"Maybe she got lost in the crowd," I stated.

"In the bathroom?" He asked doubtfully. "We found her body this morning and it's not pretty. Her body was torn apart as if she was mauled by an animal."

"Do you have a suspect?" I asked.

"Larissa Campton, a newly turned vampire."

"What proof do you have?"

"Video footage."

"Address?" I asked, tossing the wet cloth onto the table behind me.

"Unknown but she takes her victims from Blue Pulse every night. Every one of them had brown hair."

"So you want us to play bait," I stated. "I'll do it. How much is she worth?"

"Ten thousand."

"Not bad. Twice as much as last night's hunt," I surmised. "I'll take it."

"Good. Give me a call when you're done."

"I always do."

When I turned back around, I found all my friends standing there, looking at me expectedly.

"Looks like we're going clubbing, girls."

~ X ~

Upon entering, I was hit by pounding music and the strong smell of perfumes, sweat and sex. I looked back at my backup. Chelsea wore a black turtleneck dress with long sleeves that hugged her torso but once it reached mid-waist, puffed out with tulle in a tutu like fashion. The outfit was finished up with black ankle boots with a zip on the outside and thigh high stockings.

Tori was sporting a dark blue and red flannel shirt tucked into your classic black jeans and black knee high boots.

I myself wore white skinny jeans with a classy cream coloured leather, long sleeved jacket complete with silver jewelled stilettos.

I spotted Bethany drinking at the bar wearing a white cocktail dress with a black sash that tied at the back, playing the bait.

Due to Larissa's attack on humans, we knew she'd never go for vampires, so Bethany offered in our place. She's a lot stronger than the girl a met a couple years ago and I knew she could look after herself, though I was still reluctant to let her play bait but she's as stubborn as a mule.

I nodded to Chelsea and Tori who nodded back and we split up. I headed to the dance floor as Tori went to the bathroom and Chelsea to the bar. We blended in quite well, considering it's not unnatural for vampires to mix amongst humans. As I was surveying the floor, one of my favourite songs came on and I began to move with it.

Swaying with the music, I let a smile grace my lips. The lights seemed to pulse with the beat and everything seemed to blur away. I hadn't realised just how much tension I had been carrying. As the song went on, I felt myself becoming more and more relaxed. It felt like my heartbeat was in synch with the bass and my body moved to tell the story of the song. I couldn't help but to sing along to the song. Everything became distorted until it was just me and the-

"Mary!" Bethany's voice rung in my head.

My eyes snapped open and it was if reality crashed back into place.

'Shit, Bethany!' I cursed myself.

I ran from the crowd, feeling panic rise within me. What *was* that? I never -and I mean *never*- lost focus on a hunt. Tori and Chelsea joined me as we left the club, following Bethany and Larissa's presence. Both were equally as confused and flustered as I. We could feel Bethany fighting back with everything that she had but it wasn't going to be enough if we didn't get there in time.

As we burst into a park, I spotted Larissa hovering over Bethany who was bleeding quite heavily from her shoulder and I felt my mind beginning to lose focus. Everything became a haze and I felt like I was dreaming again. Just like in the club.

'Bethany needs us!' A familiar yet foreign voice screamed inside my head, clearing my mind.

When I came to, angry would have been an understatement. I held onto the stability of the voice that seemed to be immune to Larissa's mind numbing abilities.

I growled as I leapt for Larissa, tackling her off Bethany. She hissed at me and I hissed back, baring my elongated fangs and I saw the faintest hint of fear in her eyes. It brought me nothing but glee. She *should* be scared.

"You're the Rogue," she spat.

'The what?'

"You are the rogue vampire that hunts down your own kind- no. Not your own kind. You're a disgusting half-breed!" She snarled.

I slammed my fist so hard into her face repeatedly that her skull caved in. Blood and brain matter splattered onto my clothes, ruining the outfit.

I heard Tori and Chelsea behind me, groaning as they came back from the illusion Larissa had cast. They looked at me and Larissa, before going to Bethany and licking her wounds since vampire saliva holds strong healing components.

Bethany herself was a bit shaken up but she'd be okay.

"Can we go home?" She asked shakily.

-X-

"So you're telling me she called you *'The Rogue?'*" Brenton asked.

We all sat on the crescent sofa with my mobile on loud speaker. I had called him in after the deed was done but didn't stick around to welcome him to the crime scene. As soon as I hung up, we all headed straight home. We're having a group meeting. Well, *if* you could call this a group meeting. We were sitting on the couch watching cartoons, for Bethany's benefit of course.

"That's what she said," I hesitated.

Brenton laughed over the phone. "Looks like you have built a name for yourself," he said. "I'll look into my sources about *'The Rogue'* and I'll tell you what I come up with."

"Thanks. Recognition will not go down well if that's the case. How am I supposed to kill unsuspecting vampires if they suspect me?"

Brenton laughed again. "Not my problem. Goodnight," he said and the dial tone was heard.

"What a dick," I sighed as I leant back, slouching on the sofa and stared up at the large TV before turning to my elemental friend. "How're you doing, Bethany?" I asked.

"Better. I was just in shock, I think," she replied.

"We're so sorry," Tori muttered, disappointed in herself. "We didn't know that she could cast illusions."

"Don't be sorry," Cassidy stated. "How *could* you have known?"

"She must have been created from a True Born. That would explain why her ability," Reign said. "She obviously wasn't strong enough to be a True Born herself."

"But what I want to know is how were you able to break free from her ability?" Chelsea asked, turning to me.

I frowned. "I have no idea."

It was the truth, I had no idea how I snapped out of it the second time.

"What do you remember?" Cassidy asked.

"After we entered the clearing, my mind became fuzzy and I felt like I was dreaming, like I had nothing to worry about. Then a voice screamed at me that Bethany needed me and it was like I crashed into the ground, jolting awake. I held onto the power of the voice as I fought and killed Larissa," I explained.

My friends all looked at each other. "Maybe your father had a resistant ability that you inherited?" Sera asked.

"That's a possibility," Cassidy agreed.

I shrugged. "Maybe."

My family was a tough subject, my father especially. I adored my father. He obviously had it rough in order to be with my Mom. He was not a bad man, even though I believed all True Born to be arseholes. Most of them were stuck up, selfish pricks but if my father was one, he's the only exception unless someone proves me wrong but what are the chances? A fucking Turned called me disgusting. I can't imagine what the True Born would be like.

I don't envy the life my father lived.

3

Clandestine Academia

"**M**ARY?" A SOFT VOICE ASKED.

My eyes opened and I looked around groggily before focusing on Sera at the door.

"Yeah?" I mumbled, wiping my eyes.

"Can I come in?" She asked.

"Yeah," I answered as I sat up.

She entered and stood near my bed. I looked at her strangely before patting the spot next to me. She climbed onto my bed and I looked at her.

"What is it? Are the girls fighting again?" I asked.

She shook her head and I heard a slight sniffle. She was looking away from me so I turned her head towards me and saw her puffy, red eyes. She'd been crying.

"What's wrong?" I asked.

Her face scrunched up and her eyes welled with tears before she buried her head into my chest and cried. Automatically, my arms wrapped around her comfortingly. I murmured soothing words to her, trying to calm her down enough to talk to me. She cried for quite some time before she was sniffling again. Even though she was done, she didn't move away.

"What's up? Is it your family? Is Baryon giving you shit again?" I asked.

Sera's family treats her badly, namely her step-father, Baryon and her half-sister, Roseanna. Her mother, Pur, had died not long after giving birth to Roseanna. Pur's father -Sera's grandfather, Percy- was the Tima clan leader and arranged for Pur and Baryon to marry when her first husband, Kailin, was killed in one of their festive hunts.

Pur and Baryon's marriage was not a loving one, from what Sera heard from her people and he's never treated Sera well.

The bastard has been trying to replace Sera as heiress but to do so he needs to address the other clans under Draconis for approval. Thankfully, they saw no reason for him to do so and now the only way to replace her is if she dies or gives up her position as heiress willingly.

So Baryon treats her like crap in hopes that she'd just give it up but we encouraging her to fight for it.

"Baryon," she began. "He's sending me to Clandestine Academia," she said and I pulled back in shock.

Clandestine Academia was a prestigious learning institute for maturing Ascuns that have a high standing in society, like heirs and heiresses or other high positions. That doesn't stop other, lower ranking beings from going, though few go because of the school's system, the student body weed out the weak.

Seraphina was screwed if she went alone.

~ X ~

We all had a group meeting again, this time, in the kitchen at the dining table.

"So what are we going to do? We can't just let Sera go in on her own," Cassidy pleaded.

"Her gentle nature will be seen as a weakness and she will be targeted," Reign agreed.

"She'll die-" Chelsea started.

"Goddamn it, I know!" I yelled.

Everyone quieted down.

"Don't you think I know what will happen once Sera steps a foot on those grounds? The students of that school will target her. I know that already!"

I slammed my fists down on the desk angrily.

"Then, what are we going to do?" Tori asked softly.

No one said anything.

"I'll go with her," I stated.

Six pairs of eyes widened as they looked at me.

"You can't!" Cassidy yelled.

"You're a dhampir, Mary. They'll kill you, too!" Chelsea stressed out.

"I'm not letting Sera go to Clandestine Academia by herself."

"If you go, then so do we!" Reign said stubbornly.

I shook my head. "Reign-"

"No. We're going with you," Tori said, cutting me off.

"Thank you so much," Sera sniffed. "I don't want you guys to get hurt because of me but I also don't want to go alone…"

"Don't worry," Cassidy comforted her. "You know we can handle it."

"How do you plan on getting onto the Clandestine Academia enrolment list?" Chelsea asked.

We all paused to think about it for a second.

"You didn't think about that, did you?" Cassidy asked.

"Not at all," I stated sheepishly.

They all groaned and rolled their eyes. Just then, my phone started ringing. I pulled it out and answered. "Talk to me."

"Guess who?"

I rolled my eyes. "What are you, five?"

"I called to tell you about the whole '*Rogue*' thing," Brenton spoke. "But if you're going to be like that—"

"I'm listening."

"Rumour on the streets is that there's a vampire hunting her own kind. Those who feed to kill are wary of you," he said. "Though they have no idea who you are or what you look like."

It was small but a blessing none the less.

"Thanks for the information."

"No problem."

I was about to hang up when I remembered. "Brenton, wait!" I exclaimed.

"What?"

"Do you think you could get me and my friends into Clandestine Academia?"

"*You* want to go to *Clandestine Academia*?"

"Yeah. Sera's being forced to go and we don't want her to go by herself. So we're following her into Clandestine Academia, though we have no idea how to get onto the enrolment list," I told him.

"Well, your friends shouldn't really have a problem. It's just *you* my connections are going to struggle with, being a dhampir and all."

I frowned. "Do you think it can be done?"

"It *will* be done," he promised.

"Thank you."

"You're welcome. Just…be careful, 'kay?"

"Of course."

It looks like the girls' and I were good to go. I mean it's not what you know, but who you know, right?

-X-

I drifted around a bend with Chelsea laughing in the front seat and Tori cheering in the back seat of my purple Suzuki Swift. Sera followed, only slower, with Reign, Cassidy and Bethany in her baby blue Mini Cooper. I had a need for speed and my girls knew it.

My hair whipped around me as I hit the accelerator, going well over the speed limit. We were headed south east of Brisbane city towards a town called Redlands. No one lived around there as it was only trees. It was a beautiful place if you liked that kind of thing.

We reached a school called Capalaba State College. It was a normal college during the day but come night time, spells went up that kept the ignorant away. Pulling up in the car park, Chelsea, Tori and I climbed out of my car and stood there, waiting for Sera, who pulled in a few minutes later. Once they were out, we headed to the administration together.

Upon entering the school, condescending looks were immediately sent my way from the vampires. Understandable though. When was the last time a dhampir willingly attended their school?

Once we found the office, we entered and found another guy waiting. He had dark brown hair and blue eyes that almost froze me stiff. He was incredibly handsome and looking right at me.

He smirked at me before I turned my head away. We waited patiently for the administrator to finish flirting with this devilishly handsome vampire before I sensed Tori and Chelsea getting agitated and I wasn't fairing any better, nor do I think the guy was.

"-my house sometime," she finished, batting her eyelashes flirtatiously but to me, she looked like she was having a seizure with her eyes.

"Excuse me?" I said, butting in.

They both looked at me and I saw the disgust flash through the woman's eyes. Oh, I see.

"What?" She asked.

"We're the new students," I stated.

It definitely wasn't cheap, whoever Brenton's contact was. He charged me five grand for the girls and twenty for me. Fucking tight-ass but he kept his word and got us on the enrolment list.

"You're joking," she sneered before peering at her computer. "There's no way a half-breed got...into..." She stopped and I could only guess she saw our enrolment details.

"Hm? What?" Tori asked, smiling smugly at her.

She huffed and opened her mouth when someone interrupted her.

"Carla, that's enough."

We turned to see a woman walk out of a room with a few boys. She had a big chest and small waist and wore a professional outfit of a black pencil skirt and white blouse with black heels.

"I am Lady Camilla. I'm the Head Mistress of Clandestine Academia," she introduced herself.

'Camilla, really? Could you get anymore cliché?' I wondered.

"I've heard a lot about you from my brother, Tyler, who is a friend of Brenton Xander," Camilla stated.

'So that's how the bastard got us into Clandestine Academia.'

"I've heard a lot about you, Mary," she continued. "My brother explained everything to me but there are a few things I must talk to you about," she said before looking at the boys in front of her, all of them around my age. "You boys wait for me outside, alright?"

The boys nodded before one of them saluted. "Yes ma'am."

"Don't be a smart arse, Leo. Now all four of you, wait for me in the hallway."

They wordlessly left before she regarded the man at the front desk. "Mr Rubyvale, how can I help you?" Camilla asked.

The guy looked at her before bowing slightly. "I just came to collect some papers for Ms Shores but Miss Carmichael was side-tracked by retelling her weekend to me," the guy said.

Camilla turned her eyes to Carla who had the audacity to blush. She handed him the papers he must have requested earlier before he turned to leave.

"Hold on a second, Mr Rubyvale. Could you also wait out in the hallway for me?" Camilla asked.

The guy nodded before he stepped out of the office, though we could still see him and the four other boys in the hallway since the door was transparent glass. We watched as two of the guys were rough housing before one of them tackled the other to the ground and they wrestled around. Camilla sighed and shook her head before looking at us.

"First rule is, no weapons," she said. "I know you are used to fighting with them but you can't have them with you. You may have them while in HPE."

Cassidy and Reign only had one each and they placed them on the bench. Sera and Bethany shook their heads, having no weapons at all. Then Camilla looked at Tori, Chelsea and I. We sighed and started placing our weapons on the table. Chelsea pulled out her Damned Twins, plug bayonets, three daggers and a switchblade. Tori pulled out a shotgun and two pistols and I put down my Premiums and Desert Eagle. Camilla and Holly were looking at us with wide eyes before a loud bang diverted our attention.

We looked back at the boys and saw the two boys that had been wrestling were replaced by two large wolves. One had light brown fur under it and darker brown on top while the other had snow white fur underneath and light brown fur at the top.

Camilla rushed out and when the door closed, her yelling was silenced. We watched as the two wolves changed back before Camilla re-entered with the group of men.

"Boys, introduce yourselves," she snapped.

"I'm Jye," one began.

Jye had blond highlights in his brown hair that hung in his eyes which he brushed to one side and light brown eyes. He also had snake bite piercings.

"Leo," the next guy answered.

He was slightly shorter then Jye but had a bigger chest and was very broad across the shoulders. He also had a tan with many scars on his body, while Jye had none. His hair was light brown and his eyes were dark, almost black. His left cheek was scarred, too.

"Blade."

Blade had a darker tan than I and a small, dark brown afro. He had a well-toned body and I knew he was probably the strongest of the wolf boys. He was one of the ones wrestling as was the next one who smiled politely.

"I'm Kalum," he introduced himself.

He was smaller than the others but I bet he was the fastest. He had gel spiked, light brown hair and hazel brown eyes.

All of the boys were missing shirts so we could clearly see just how much they worked out. Then we turned to the vampire who gave a slight smile. He took my hand and bowed.

"Alistair Rubyvale," was all he said before his lips touched my knuckles.

I felt myself beginning to flush.

"These men will be your escorts for the week to ensure you make it to your classes on time," she said before she handed each of us girls a piece of paper. "Here are your class schedules. You all selected your electives though some of your classes are different since you're of different species," Camilla explained.

The girls and I nodded.

"Alright, Jye, you'll be Chelsea and Tori's escort. Kalum, you'll be Seraphina's. Blade, you'll go with Cassidy and Reign. Leo, you'll be with Bethany and Mr Rubyvale, you'll take Mary. Is that clear?" Camilla asked.

The boys nodded. Camilla nodded her head before walking back into the office. The girls and I looked at our time table.

"I have music," I said.

"We'll take you to your classes," Blade offered and they started to go their separate ways.

I caught Kalum before he went too far. "Please take care of Sera for me. I was hoping I'd be targeted but I'm scared that by not being there, they'd settle for her," I pleaded.

Kalum nodded. "Don't worry, I'll look after her," he said.

"Thank you."

I hugged Sera and slipped a silver blade into her pocket. Her eyes widened slightly.

"For protection," I explained.

"Mary-"

"Please, just take it," I murmured. "I'll feel better knowing you have this with you."

She sighed but nodded. "A-Alright."

"Thank you."

She turned and walked off with Kalum. I nodded to the others and they smiled back. I knew they had weapons still hidden somewhere on them and I wondered if Camilla knew. I turned to look through the office glass walls and saw her standing there, staring at us. Oh yeah, she definitely knew.

4

Supernatural Studies

A LISTAIR AND I WALKED DOWN the silent hallway, passing a few doors until we finally stopped at one. We all missed form class so we went to our first lesson.

"This is the music block. Sometimes we like to be loud, so we spread out into other rooms since no one else but us use them," Alistair explained.

He knocked on the door and an elegant woman with blue-black hair and ocean blue eyes opened the door. She was beautiful.

"Ah, Alistair, you're late," she said as she took the papers from him.

Her voice was soft and kind, reminding me of Sera.

"I was being assigned to escort a new student," Alistair explained.

His tone was a tenor, like my dad. He was polite too and was neither snobby nor condescending. It felt like velvet silk caressing my ears.

"A new student, what a pleasant surprise," she said happily as she stepped aside to let us in.

Upon entering the room, I spotted only a few other people in this class; three guys and one female.

"You're part of this class?" I asked Alistair, who nodded.

"My name is Michelle Shores. What's yours?" The teacher asked.

"Mary," I answered.

"What instrument do you play?" She asked.

I blushed. "I don't actually play an instrument. I've always wanted to, though. My dad played the piano and my mom accompanied him with a cello or violin," I said. "I was hoping to follow in their footsteps."

"That's okay. I'll teach you the basics of piano first and then we'll see how you go, alright?" She asked and I nodded. "Everyone, this is Mary. She's a new student so be nice."

The other four occupants glared at me. I rolled my eyes. This was really getting old.

The class broke up so as to spread out and play their separate instruments in peace. Meanwhile, I took a seat with Alistair beside me and listened to what Michelle was telling me about the scales and keys then she had me give it a go. I smiled when I played the scales the way she wanted me to. She smiled down at me.

"You have potential," Alistair spoke.

"Hey, Alistair," the other female called, smiling seductively. "I'm having trouble with one of my songs on the flute. Could you help me?" She asked.

She had long, blonde hair and sparkling blue eyes. She was a vampire, as were the other three in this class. Her voice was Soprano, light and formal. She never openly insulted me but her tone said it all.

"I find it hard to believe that you're having trouble, Angela," Alistair spoke smoothly.

I felt a shiver run down my spine but he turned and left anyway.

"Alright Mary, when you go home, find a song you want to learn to play and I'll help you, okay?" Michelle asked.

I smiled and nodded as the bell went. I stood and Alistair walked back in to me. I picked up the book Michelle had given me for music and turned to him. He was staring down at me and I felt my cheeks begin to flush.

"You don't mind if I stop by my friend's car, do you? I have a bag with a few books in her boot, just in case," I said. "Now that I know I need them, I'd like to grab them."

He agreed and led the way out. Along the way, I met up with the other girls and their escorts.

"You came to collect your bags too?" I asked and they nodded.

"I can't believe I'm in school again," Tori groaned.

I shrugged. "It's not that different from the human high school I attended."

"Yeah," Bethany agreed. "The only difference is that we're studying supernatural subjects."

We got to the car park where Sera popped her boot open and we all grabbed our bag packs. I didn't use my own because weapons were occupying it. You could never be too careful.

"What do you have now?" Kalum asked.

"I have Ancient History of Vampires," I said.

"Same," Tori and Chelsea said in unison.

The second bell went, telling us we were late.

"Come on, we're going to be late," Tori said before pausing. "You know what, take your time."

I laughed at her before we split again, this time Jye and Alistair were leading. I watched as they talked quietly amongst themselves when Chelsea elbowed me.

"What?" I asked.

"You were totally checking Alistair out."

I blushed brightly. "I was not," I snapped. "If you must know, oh so *knowledgeable* one, I was trying to hear what they were saying?"

"Uh huh, sure," both drawled.

We reached our classroom and I saw Jye frown before we opened the door. It's basic knowledge to know that vampires and werewolves hate each other. I kind of see them as normal people that just so happen to turn into an oversized wolf once or so a month. Nothing out of the ordinary. Then again, this is coming from a dhampir, one who was brought up as an outcast.

When the door opened, every pair of eyes turned to us. The room was huge and holding at least thirty or so vampires. There were four classes each subject. I'm just glad that I got Tori *and* Chelsea in mine.

"Sorry we're late Mr Wrath. The girls had to grab their possessions from their car," Alistair explained.

Mr Wrath (Konan Wrath, it said on my schedule) was a tall, very intimidating looking man. He had light brown hair and piercing black eyes.

He glared down at us. "Fine then. Since you three are new students, how about you introduce yourself to the class?" He asked before taking a seat at the front of the class.

Alistair took his seat and I turned to Jye who looked like he wanted to be anywhere but here.

"Just leave already, mutt-face," a guy called.

At least half of the vampires laughed, Alistair not being one of them. The guy that called out was bigger than me and had red hair. Jye growled dangerously.

"Do you mind?" I asked and the laughing stopped.

"The fuck did you say, whore?" He growled.

Tori took a threatening step towards him, but I grabbed her shoulder.

"You heard her, you fat fuck," Tori snapped.

"Enough. Mr Mac, stay in for detention," Konan interrupted.

The guy's last name is Mac? Really? He'd make for the perfect McDonald's mascot. Tori started snickering and I knew she thought the same thing as me. Wicked minds think alike...or was that genius minds?

"I thought you were going to try and keep out of trouble on the first day?" Chelsea reprimanded.

"He started it," Tori defended.

I turned to Jye. "You can go do whatever for now and come back later if you like. I'm sure that would beat being in here with all these vampires," I offered.

He gave me a grateful look and I smiled in response. He said nothing though as he turned and left. Before the door completely closed behind him, I just caught sight of him changing and taking off down the hall before the door obscured my view.

"Introduce yourselves, quickly," Konan snapped.

Tori stepped forward. "My name is Victoria Graves but my friends call me Tori," she said before stepping back and Chelsea took her place.

"I'm Chelsea Amaranthine."

I stepped forward. "And I am Mary Hazel."

"Why are you here, half-breed?" A boy asked.

"None of your business," Chelsea stated.

"Take a seat," Konan said gruffly.

Tori and Chelsea took the two empty seats near McFaggot. I looked around to find other empty seats littered around the large classroom. There was another next to Alistair and I knew no one would try anything when he was around me. Not to say that I couldn't defend myself.

"Now that that's over, Emma, keep reading," Konan ordered.

A girl I couldn't spot thanks to all the heads in the way did as she was told and read from her textbook. I sighed but listened to what was being read out.

"I told you this was a bad idea," Chelsea muttered in my mind.

I smirked but looked over at Alistair's text book that I hadn't noticed he had gotten out. He raised an eyebrow and I blushed before I looked at the book, wanting to look as if I was paying attention.

"Mary, you're totally crushing," Tori stated and the two snickered.

"Do you mind? I'm trying to pay attention," Bethany's voice invaded our minds.

25

Because of Chelsea's blood, we were all connected. We could keep our minds to ourselves if we wanted to. It's almost like an automatic door in our minds. You walk to the door and it'll open. Once you pull yourself out of that shared room, the door automatically closes behind you so you always have your privacy and separate mind.

"You? Paying attention?" Chelsea asked.

"Hey!" Bethany yelled and we all snickered.

"Mary, Wrath's talking to you," Tori warned.

My eyes snapped up to find Konan's face red, glaring daggers at me with a horrible scowl upon his face.

"If you're not going to pay attention, leave my class," he snapped.

"Don't you dare," Tori and Chelsea threatened.

I sighed but nodded my head. "I'm sorry, sir," I apologised. "It won't happen again."

His scowl didn't fade, "It better not, Hazel," he growled.

I nodded and he continued on.

"Talk to you guys at lunch," I sighed. *"Teach looks like he's about to blow a fuse."*

I didn't wait for their response when I came out of our mental chat room. I looked up at Alistair who nodded his head to me before looking back at Mr Hothead. What the hell was that nod supposed to mean? God, this guy is so freaking hard to understand.

An hour later, I was almost falling asleep. Ancient History of Vampires was just as boring as Ancient History at the human high school I graduated from two years ago. I would give almost anything for this lesson to be over.

The bell rang.

Jye entered then but Chelsea and I bolted out the door, grabbing an arm each and dragging him down the hallway. Once we were a safe distance away, we let Jye go.

"What the fuck?" He asked us.

"That class was shit," I huffed.

"We have Vampire Studies next," Alistair stated, amused.

I frowned before I felt my phone vibrating. Alistair led the way to our next class as I pulled out my phone and answered it.

"Talk to me."

"How's your first day of school?" Brenton asked.

"Horrible. It's just like high school, only I'm surrounded by supernatural beings."

"Sounds fun."

"Bite me."

"Sorry babe, that's your job," he teased.

I rolled my eyes.

"But speaking of jobs, I've got a hunt for you tonight," he stated.

"Thank god, something that resembles my old life," I exaggerated.

Brenton laughed. "If only you were always this eager."

"I *am* always this eager," I stated flatly.

"Touché."

"What's the job?" I asked.

"We believe there are a few vampires hiding in the underground train tunnels. The train goes in, a few people don't come out," Brenton stated.

"How many do you think there might be?"

"Between three to five."

"We'll take care of it tonight."

"I knew you would but not until you finish your homework."

"You son of a-"

He hung up.

"Prick," I hissed.

"Is it a good hunt?" Tori asked.

"I believe it is," I stated.

"How many?" Chelsea asked.

"Three to five."

"Fun," Chelsea said, smirking.

"What's this 'hunt' you're talking about?" Jye asked.

"Nothing," the three of us said in unison, smiling at each other.

The second bell rang and I groaned. We stood outside the door to our next class. Tori, Chelsea and I hung our heads as Alistair opened the door.

For once, I couldn't wait until tonight to spill some blood. At least you can fight against vamps and win. You can't fight boredom and expect to come out on top. It just doesn't happen.

5

Dying To Fit In

"Oh my god, how hot was Mr Nightingale?" Tori asked.

"Meh," Chelsea shrugged.

I looked up at Alistair who walked a little ahead of us while Tori tried to convince Chelsea that Richard Nightingale, our Vampire Studies teacher, was the hottest teacher at the school while Jye followed behind. Sure, he was hot but he couldn't hold a candle to Alistair.

I shook my head. It's the first day of Clandestine Academia and I'm sounding like a love struck fool. Pathetic.

"Thank god it's lunch time," I sighed.

Alistair looked back at me and I looked away as butterflies fluttered in my stomach.

"Hey, Mary," Tori called, catching my attention.

I turned to her. "Yeah?"

"Chelsea and I are going to check out the gymnasium training room. See what they got, you know," Tori explained. "Want to come?"

"Nah, I'll meet up with the others," I declined. "You two go ahead."

They nodded and Jye led them away. I followed Alistair out to the darkened courtyard where everyone was socialising.

There were many tables outside where they were but many more were standing around, chatting. There were a few fairies were sitting in a tree -Sera being one of them- to the left of the courtyard. A few elementals -including Bethany- sat near them. Cassidy and Reign were doing the same, only at a different table with angels. They all fit in so well.

I rubbed my glove-covered arm self-consciously. What did I expect? Hugs and friendly smiles from everyone? Maybe if they're hiding knives behind their backs.

Alistair led me to a table where I saw a few other vampires.

"Hey Ali!" A blonde called out.

He had sparkling blue eyes, a lean body and long blond hair in a ponytail. He was cute and very feminine looking. Beside him was a guy with spiky, auburn hair and green eyes. He was shorter with the same build only his eyes were dull with boredom and disinterest. There was a large brunette who was seriously packing in the protein. He looked like a walking, talking, *breathing* brick wall with beady black eyes.

The last two were a couple; you could see it in the way they looked at each other. The girl had short, dyed cerulean blue hair and brown eyes. She had a nose and tongue piercing as well. She was gorgeous and she went well with her boyfriend who had snake bites and a piercing on his right eyebrow. He had dyed red hair and stormy blue eyes. I loved them already.

"Ali?" I asked Alistair, who glared at the blonde.

"Everyone, this is Mary," Alistair said and I gave a small wave. "Mary, this is William, Rolan, Brock, Aura and Mikai."

They nodded to me.

"What's up?" Rolan asked.

"A hybrid," Mikai stated. "You've got guts coming here. I respect that."

"Looks like the kitten has claws," Brock teased.

"Shut up, Tiny."

"Tiny? Me?" He asked, flexing his muscles.

"I wasn't talking about your muscles," I shot back, smirking and his smug grin fell before he growled threateningly.

I knew that sound. I heard it all too often. I crouched into a defensive stance as his growling increased in volume. Before I drew out a knife, it broke into laughter. I stood rigid, looking at him in confusion.

"You're a tough one, Kitten. I like you," he said, still laughing.

"Thank you?"

"Don't mind him, he's....special," Aura laughed before I felt someone grab my hair.

I was dragged backwards a couple metres before the person who held my hair tossed me into the dirt. I looked up to see a girl I had never met before.

"Get out of here hybrid!" She yelled at me. "Not only do you come and taint our school, you go and bother Alistair too, even if he hangs out with the freak shows," she scowled.

"The fuck did you say?!" Aura yelled but Mikai held her back.

I got up and dusted myself off before I slapped her. She stumbled back and held her cheek that sported four scratch marks due to my nails.

"I'm not leaving until my friend does, so get used to me!" I snapped and shoved her into the nearest advancing vampire.

Many had formed a circle around me, all hissing threateningly. It's the same with werewolves. If someone doesn't like you, they'll challenge you. If you win, you're considered above them on the leader board. The only difference is that vampires kill their challengers.

My fangs lengthened and I hissed back. Then the brawl started. I dodged under someone's fist but another scratched me across the face. I turned to see it was the same girl from before. An eye for an eye. Brown eyes bled to red as blood ran down my cheek. My nails elongated to claws and I snarled angrily.

Suddenly, I wasn't alone. I could feel people around me, almost touching. I turned my head to see my friends. Cassidy and Reign had their feathered wings out on display. Cassidy's were gold while Reign's shone baby blue. Seraphina stood at the rear, her purple wings glittering in the moonlight. The pink and green designs within seemed to glow. Bethany stood with her arms outstretched, ready to conjure up a hurricane if need be.

"So the hybrid has friends," the girl sneered.

"I was just thinking, if I killed you right now, would that make the others back down?"

"Talk is cheap, half-breed," she hissed. "Don't threaten me."

"It's not a threat. It's a promise," I growled coldly.

She screeched and launched herself at me but she never made it. A hand grabbed her by her hair, plucking her out of the air and forcing her to the ground. It was Chelsea.

"What's going on here?" Tori asked cheerily.

"I don't know, but it looks like fun," Chelsea stated. "It seems to me that this one tried to attack or friends."

She regarded the vampire caught in her grasp.

"Is that so?" Tori asked. "Well if that's true, we just saved your life."

"Let me go!" She screeched.

Chelsea shook her by the hair. "Keep it down, bitch."

"Let her go," I sighed, wiping the blood from my face, wincing as I touched the scratches.

It kept bleeding so I gave up. Chelsea shrugged and released her. The girl staggered forward before whirling around, ready to fight.

"You want to fight me? Fine. But it's one on one, you fucking cowards," I hissed.

They snarled.

"Whatever," the girl hissed. "I don't need them to kill a fucking half-breed," she snapped before pouncing again.

"Go, Tama!" Someone shouted from the crowd.

When she brought her claws down upon me, I caught her wrist before it could make contact. I smirked at her and snapped her wrist as easily as snapping a twig. She howled in pain but I only spun into her so I had her in an arm lock and snapped it at the elbow. She screamed louder and I spun out and watched her. She cradled her right arm that I had broken as she whimpered.

"You were saying?" I asked and she hissed at me.

"Go to hell!" She screeched and I instantly had her other arm.

"Guess what happens next?"

She shook her head before I broke her left arm in the same places as the right. She started crying before I had her in a head lock.

"Give up?" I asked.

"Fuck you!" She spat, though her shaking made me almost pity her.

I snapped her neck and let her body drop to the ground. Almost.

"Who's next?" I asked.

I heard some guy yell and dodged to the side when he brought down a sword to where I was just standing. Swords now?

"How come you get a weapon?" I asked.

He only yelled as he continued to swing at me with the sword.

"That's a nice sword. Dibs," Chelsea called.

I caught the sword with my left hand in the exact same place as my scar from previously trying to stop a sword with my hand.

"Yeah, sure," I paused, smirking at the guy. "Dead people don't need swords," I stated before pulling the sword from him.

His eyes widened before the sword was thrust into his stomach. He looked down at sword that impaled him. My hand followed the sword into his body and I ripped out his heart.

I pulled the sword from his corpse and he crumpled to the ground like Tama.

"I didn't even catch your name," I stated to myself. "Oh well."

I dropped his heart on his chest and tossed the sword to Chelsea who smiled at it. She gave it a few test swings.

"Love it," Chelsea answered.

"Who's next?" I asked before someone grabbed Bethany around the neck.

"It seems you know how to protect yourself better than any of the half-breeds who came here before you so we may have to use a different method," he stated.

"That is a very bad idea," Tori stated.

"One move and she gets it," he threatened.

Bethany who was going red in the face with anger. Her eyes turned a shimmering, silver-lavender. The guy winced and pushed her away from him as the wind began to pick up. She turned and glared at him with her eyes still glowing. He started shouting in pain and eventually, his chest exploded from the air being forced into his lungs like a balloon. Blood, bone and guts sprayed us like a shower as the bell rang.

"Yuck," Sera shuddered.

"Well, that was fun," Reign said before looking at Bethany whose eyes had faded back to blue. "How are you doing?"

"Good. I'm not feeling too bad."

"You're improving," Tori acknowledged.

The crowd began to disperse, some sending us glares, others avoiding my eyes and some just scared shitless.

"Time for class," Aura spoke as she and the others approached us.

"Oh, right," I said. "Everyone, these are Alistairs' friends. This is Aura, her boyfriend Mikai, William, Rolan and Tiny," I stated.

"Fuck you, Kitten," Brock growled.

"No, thank you."

"Come on, we all have HPE," William rushed, but he grabbed my face in his hands. "You poor girl," he said before he licked my blood off my cheek, healing the wound.

His eyes darkened instantly. Tori and Chelsea were between us in a second, holding him back. Rolan merely came along and gave him a good smack across the back of his head.

"Ow! Rolan," he whined.

"Shut up, idiot. You looked ready to pounce on the girl," Rolan said, frowning.

"Oh, I get it," William cooed, smiling smugly. "You're jealous."

"Whatever. Just get your ass to class," Rolan scowled, dragging William off with him.

We could only watch in amusement.

"Are they a couple?" Sera asked, looking at us with such innocence.

"It's complicated. Rolan's gay and William is bisexual," Aura said. "William likes to experiment and tease Rolan so Rolan sleeps with a lot of men to piss William off."

"Oh my god, that's adorable," Tori squealed.

"Alright, let's go to HPE," Chelsea sighed and started to walk off.

They all turned to follow, as did I, when I caught sight of a girl by the bushes. She had glowing blue eyes and sandy blond hair. She was gorgeous but it was like she could see right through me. She stared at me and I stared right back.

"Mary," it was Cassidy who had called me and brought me out of my staring contest.

I turned to see the others had been waiting for me.

"You okay?" Tori asked.

I looked back to find the girl was gone like she was never there.

"Yeah," I muttered. "Fine."

I followed them to the large gymnasium, thinking only about that girl. Was I seeing things? Who was she?

6

THE VOICE

W E GOT TO THE GYMNASIUM and the first thing I noticed was that half the school was here. Everyone had HPE at the same time and there were only two classes of HPE, meaning more people per class. My friends and I were in the A-class. A man approached us so I assumed he was our teacher.

"Oh, the new girls. I heard you killed three vampires at lunch," he said. "My name is Timothy Thora and I am your HPE teacher."

"Nice to meet you," I stated, nodding.

Looking around, I noticed the teachers had been split up as well, so half were with us and the other would be in the B-Class. Timothy seemed to notice we had the attention of those around and us and addressed the matter at hand.

"Please go back to what you were doing," he asked of the students.

When none of them moved, I felt a sinister power lash out from him and his hazel green eyes flashed crimson.

"I said go back to what you were doing!" He roared, his voice deeper and darker.

Everyone quickly did as they were told. When he turned back to us, his eyes were back to their hazel colour.

"Here, everyone is taught how to fight within their elements. You'll be taught something and practice it with your friends if you wish," he said.

We nodded and Tori, Chelsea and I followed Aura who led us to Michelle, my music teacher. We were to choose a teacher we wanted to learn from and everyone went to either Konan or Richard. Alistair, Rolan, William and Mikai were with Timothy. Looking around, I found Brock with Konan.

"Oh, hello girls," Michelle greeted us.

She was definitely one of my favourite teachers.

"Hey, Michelle," I greeted back. "Girls, this is Michelle Shores. She also teaches my music class. Michelle, these are my friends, Chelsea and Tori."

"Pleased to meet you. So you wish to learn from me? I'm quite surprised," she said.

"You can tell why everyone wants to learn from Konan or Richard," Aura muttered, tone filled with disgust. "If they go to Konan, all they want is power. That's just how they are. Most of them are guys. All the girls are with Richard because he's hot."

"Stupid fan girls," Chelsea grumbled.

"Calm down, Chels," Tori laughed.

"It's just stupid!" She snapped. "Obviously, this class is to help you control your powers, not to try to get lucky with the bloody teacher."

"Is that a hint of jealousy I see dripping from your lips?" Tori teased.

"Shut up, Tori," Chelsea growled. "You know it's not that. I just don't understand how girls could prefer to spend their time throwing themselves at the teacher instead of trying to improve," Chelsea ranted. "God, no wonder why those people were so weak."

"Mm," I hummed in agreement, nodding. "You have a point."

"Don't worry too much about them," Tori said. "They're the ones that are going to die, not us."

"Again, point made," I input. "Besides, I'm pretty sure they haven't been through what we have. If they had, they would've realised that you need every advantage in life you can get and just how easily one's life can be destroyed."

"Agreed," both said in unison.

"Alright then ladies. What I have taught Aura is that while strength and speed are necessary advantages, if you cannot dodge your enemy's attacks, what chance will you get to attack back if you're already dead?" Michelle asked.

"This, we already knew," Tori stated.

"Of course. With that display of yours at lunch, I have no doubt that you have mastered the art of dodging," she agreed. "But, have you ever opened your third eye?" She asked.

The three of us remained silent.

"If you are blinded and deafened, how do you expect to fight?" Michelle asked.

No answer again.

"By opening your mind's eye, you can see and feel everything through a different light," Michelle explained.

"It's actually pretty easy," Aura put in. "But it's something almost everyone seems to have forgotten or never got the training for. Angels use their minds eye to search souls and hearts."

"So, I will first test all three of you individually in dodging. Then I will cover your eyes and see how you do, followed by covering your ears. After all three of you have been tested in your defence, Aura will do the same before showing you what happens when your minds' eye is open when you lose your senses," Michelle said. "Afterwards, I will train you all how to open it and you will keep practicing until its second nature to you."

"Sounds good," Chelsea shrugged.

"Alright, Chelsea, you're up first," Michelle said.

Chelsea nodded and walked to the large area we had near the far left corner. Every teacher had a corner. To the far right was Wrathie, front right was Richard and front left was Timothy.

"You know what you're doing?" Michelle asked.

"Defence only," Chelsea recited.

"Good," Michelle said, smiling before she disappeared from sight.

I loved watching Chelsea and Tori when they fought. Both were amazing in their own ways. Chelsea was like a dancer by the way she moved with her swords, all part of an intricate and meaningful dance. She wields her swords not just as an extension of her arms like you hear all the time on TV but as if she was part of the sword itself. It's like she adds her being into every strike, every kill. You can see her get lost in her tuneless dance of death from the moment she draws her swords to the second she returns them to their sheath.

Tori's entirely different. Where Chelsea is graceful and stealthy, Tori is overpowering and stable. You can see in her eyes the moment she touches an object, she's already thought of several way to kill you with it. When we go on hunts, the second she holds a weapon, her confidence and presence overwhelms you. She knows what she's doing and you shit yourself when you know she's ran through fifteen difference scenarios of how you die. You feel that knowledge through her aura. When she holds a weapon, you can't help but hesitate when you see her wield it with such expertise and practice, even if it's only a plastic lid off a container. You just know she can turn it into something lethal and dangerous.

Together, the two are Death's wettest dreams.

As expected, Chelsea was dancing around Michelle with graceful spins and manoeuvres. She attracted much attention and soon, there were others around us.

"Can we help you?" Tori snapped, frowning at the crowd.

They ignored her and spoke amongst themselves about us.

"I don't think you understood what I was really saying. Fuck off!" She shouted and they quickly went back to what they were doing.

Michelle was not going easy which made Tori giddy for a challenge. When Chelsea's eyes were covered, her performance barely changed from the elegant flow of clothing. The second her ears were covered, she was slightly startled. There was hardly a time where I think Chelsea lost her sense of hearing. Maybe that's why she was freaking out now. Her smooth dance became jerky and inconsistent, resulting in a few cuts and bruises. When Chelsea was knocked off her feet, Michelle ended it there by dragging a nail gently across her throat to signify she had 'killed' Chelsea.

"See? By losing your sight and hearing, you also became hesitant and started panicking, making you so much easier to kill," Michelle told us. "Other than that, you did excellent," she said.

Chelsea got up and dusted herself off before taking the blindfold and special ear plugs that she was made to wear. Already, her cuts and bruises were healed. She walked back to us.

"I've said it many times before but I'll say it again. You're amazing," Tori said.

Chelsea smiled and there was a tiny blush tainting her cheeks.

"Mary, you're next sweetheart," Michelle insisted.

I nodded and walked into the centre with Michelle. She disappeared and I slipped into my defensive stance. I sensed her behind me and dodged left, missing her kick. I flipped backwards to avoid a strike to the face. Rolling, flipping, ducking, jumping and spinning, I avoided all her attacks until she stopped me.

"Alright, good," Michelle praised. "Now we'll cover your eyes."

Chelsea tossed the blindfold to me and I put it on.

We went at it again. I felt that it didn't affect my performance. When I was with Amelia, she did the exact same thing. Soon, I was required to block my hearing and I knew this one would be tricky.

Alright. Concentrate, Mary. You can do this.

But I felt that familiar sense of panic rise in me. The same feeling I had when I was facing those vampires that murdered my parents. I may not be facing sadistic blood-suckers but I am surrounded by hybrid-haters and I knew they would kill me in my sleep if given the chance.

With the adrenaline coursing through my body, my thoughts ran a hundred miles an hour and I started to panic. I bit my lip in fear.

Shit.

I clenched my hands into fists, digging my nails into my skin. Pain brought me out of that state of panic and I took a few deep breaths.

'Dodge right.'

And I did, feeling Michelle brush passed my left shoulder. It was that voice again.

'Back flip.'

Following the orders given to me by the voice inside my head, I successfully dodged Michelle's attacks.

'Jump.'

I thought about the voice as I jumped high into the air, sensing Michelle run underneath me. It didn't sound like one of my friends, but it had to be. Normal people don't hear voices in their head and I know I'm not insane...or am I?

"Don't be stupid," I muttered out loud. "I'm not insane."

Then who the fuck was in my head?

'Seriously girls, if it's you, cut the shit. You had your fun,' I thought telepathically but no one said anything.

Checking the mental door to my head, I found it locked shut as it always is until I decide to open it. What the fuck is going on?

'Roll backwards then dive right.'

'Who the hell are you?' I cursed but received no answer.

"Let's stop there," Michelle said and I stood up straight and pulled the ear plugs and blindfold off. "Excuse me for a second," Michelle murmured before walking to Timothy.

We watched the two talked before Alistair was brought into the conversation. Then they stopped and all three turned to me. I gulped.

"Did I do something wrong?" I asked Chelsea.

"You mean besides talking to yourself while dodging perfectly? No," Chelsea answered.

"You okay, Mary?" Tori asked softly.

"Yeah, why wouldn't I be?" I asked.

Tori took my hands and showed me the blood. The cuts had already healed.

"We sensed you starting to freak out before everything went silent in your head," Tori stated.

It was quiet between us for a few seconds.

"That voice came back," I murmured.

"You mean the one that helped you with Bethany?" Chelsea asked.

"Yeah."

"What did it say?" Tori asked.

"It just told me what to do and where to go to dodge successfully," I answered.

"Does that count as cheating?"

Chelsea face palmed herself. "Tori, you're missing the point."

"Mary, can you come here for a second please?" Michelle called to me.

Chelsea, Tori and I shared a look before they nodded to me. I nodded walked to Michelle.

"I don't know of any other way to ask this but...honey, do you hear a voice in your head?" Michelle asked.

I looked at them carefully for a moment, regarding the three of them cautiously before nodding.

"When was the last time you heard this voice?" Michelle asked.

I looked to Alistair who nodded and sent me a reassuring smile.

"When I covered my ears just before," I answered.

They looked at each other again.

"What did it tell you?" Timothy asked, turning back to me.

"How to move to dodge your attacks."

"Have you heard this voice before?" Michelle asked.

"Yes, when Bethany was in trouble a few days ago. It brought me back to my senses and it seems to be immune to mind control," I said.

"No, that's not right," Timothy spoke to himself before addressing me again. "Think back further. Normally the voice develops at a young age."

"I don't think- oh..."

"Do you remember now?" Alistair asked.

"I heard the voice just after my parents died. I thought it was just an imaginary friend before my caretaker told me it was dangerous and could lead to more problems. She told me to ignore it and eventually, the voice went away."

I looked at them warily.

"Is something wrong with me?"

"Just the opposite, sweetheart," Michelle assured before looking to Timothy. "This is within your jurisdiction so I'll let you handle it," she told him before sending me a smile and heading back to Tori, Chelsea and Aura.

I went to follow but Timothy stopped me.

"You're here for now, Mary," Timothy said.

"But I wanted to watch Toris' run through."

"This is important," Alistair argued.

"Then can you please tell me what the hell's going on?"

"Mary, the voice you hear in your head is something extremely rare. It's genetic in the ancient families," he said.

"I've already guessed that my dad was from an ancient family. Only the Ancients can have children, right?"

Timothy nodded. "Precisely but only a handful of vampires from the ancient families have this inner voice in their head."

"What is this voice exactly?" I asked.

"It's the voice of your inner vampire. They are you, only full blooded, which is incredible for you since you are a half-blood," Timothy said. "It normally develops after something traumatic takes place during childhood. You and the purest of your vampire blood split and formed two people; you and your inner vampire."

"So it's me I'm hearing in my head?" I asked, trying to connect the dots.

"Yes. It's exactly like you and with the proper training, you may be able to merge back with her," Timothy said.

"What kind of proper training?"

"Many long hours of meditation," Timothy said. "Alistair, Rolan, William and I have these inner voices as well so you're not alone. But only Michelle and Camilla know of this."

"So does Mikai, Brock and Aura," William input.

"And we'd like to keep it that way," Timothy said.

"Well, my girls already know about the voice inside my head," I said. "It saved one of their lives, but they can keep a secret," I assured.

Timothy nodded. "That's fine but let's try to keep this all on the down low, alright?"

"So what do you want me to do?"

"What do you have next?" Timothy asked.

I pulled out my schedule. "A spare."

"You have a spare also, don't you, Alistair?" It was more a statement then a question. "During your spare, could you help Mary with her meditation?"

Alistair only nodded.

"Do you have to tell your friends?" Timothy asked.

"No, I'll just do it mentally," I said.

"I don't understand," William frowned.

"Chelsea holds the power of telepathy. She shared her blood with our group and took that power to a new level, being strongly connected to her mentally. Although, Tori and I need some of her blood regularly due to our bodies natural reaction to breakdown foreign substances within our bloodstream. I think that if they let me, I can get inside their head and see through their eyes," I said.

"That would be most interesting to see," Timothy murmured.

"Just out of curiosity, how did you know I had an inner voice?" I asked.

To my surprise, it was Alistair that answered instead.

"Those who are closely connected with their inner voice are able to sense when another is close by. The moment I saw you, I knew you had one. I just needed more evidence for Timothy to believe me," he said, a tiny smirk on his lips. "When Michelle told Timothy that she believed you had one, he was convinced."

He leant forward so only I could hear.

"If you hadn't noticed, he's infatuated with her."

I took a glance at Timothy to see he was now staring at Michelle who was too busy training Tori.

"I didn't notice," I whispered back.

"It doesn't matter," he stated. "Now, contact your friends and let them know what's going on."

I walked into my mental chat room and knocked on the girls' doors. I saw Tori slightly falter in the physical room before regaining control but hastily threw her mental door open so as to get back to her fight.

"Mary," Cassidy greeted. *"What's up?"*

"I have some news."

I was vaguely aware of Alistair staring at me.

"What is it?" Sera asked, worriedly. *"Are you okay?"*

"What does Timmy want with you?" Chelsea asked.

"You know that voice that I hear?" I asked.

"Yeah," they all said in unison.

"Well, apparently it's my inner vampire. After a traumatic experience, my pure vampire blood split from the rest of me and formed another being inside me. My inner vampire," I explained. *"I have to train harder so that someday, I might be able to fuse with my other half."*

"That sounds awesome," Chelsea said.

"Ah, shit!" Tori cursed as she was beaten by Michelle.

I watched her go stand next to Chelsea.

"Oh, right," I snapped. *"Tori, I also want to try and go into your head and if I'm able to see through your eyes. You know, like another passenger in your mind."*

She was silent a moment before finally she decided. *"Alright, just don't go too far into my mind."*

"Agreed."

Mentally, I walked through her door and suddenly, my vision went black.

"W-What's going on? I can't see anything!"

I felt someone holding my arms and legs down.

"Mary, can you hear me?" William asked me worriedly.

"It's alright. You've just lost your sight momentarily," Rolan explained.

"It's okay, Mary," Tori assured.

I felt her take my mental self's hand and lead me further through the darkness until finally, the darkness started to blur and give way to shapes.

When things cleared, I was staring at Chelsea.

"Chelsea?" I asked but she didn't hear me.

"I'm not Chelsea," I heard William say.

What the hell is going on?

7

INNER MEANING

"WILLIAM?" I ASKED IN CONFUSION.

I looked to the side and saw William, Rolan and Alistair standing by someone. I gasped when I realised it was me, well, my body.

"What's going on?" I wondered.

"Tori?" Chelsea asked.

"Huh?" I looked back to Chelsea to see her staring at me.

"Mary, what do you see?" Rolan asked.

"Chelsea," I answered.

He sounded like he was right above me. Looking at my body, he was.

"Mary, are you in there?" Chelsea asked.

I nodded my head.

"It worked?" Chelsea asked before looking at my body.

"Who's in control of the body?" Chelsea asked.

"I don't know," I answered but she still didn't hear me. "Why can't you hear me!?"

"Mary, your real body is talking," Alistair stated. "When you talk, it's your body that speaks, not Toris'."

"What's the point of that?" I asked, annoyed.

"I don't know but I think something went wrong when you tried to get into Toris' head," Rolan said.

"Where's Tori?" Alistair asked.

"She should be in her head with you," William stated.

I searched her mind but didn't find her. In my mind, I walked back to the door and found Tori standing outside it, pissed.

"What the hell was that!?" She yelled at me.

"What was what? Where did you go?" I asked, confused.

"You forced me out when you came in," she said and my eyes widened.

43

"I did?" I asked. "I'm so sorry. I didn't know I did it."

I grabbed her hand and pulled her in.

When I opened my eyes again, Tori was in control of her body and I was just watching everything.

"That was weird," Tori said.

She looked at my body and walked there with Chelsea.

"Mary, can you hear us still?" Alistair asked.

"So you're in Tori's head now? You solved the problem?" William asked.

"Yeah, I accidentally forced Tori out."

The bell went and Tori looked to Alistair.

"How does she go back?" Tori asked.

"Same way she went in," he said. "The hardest part was supposed to be getting into your head."

"Go back to your head now, Mary," Tori said.

I mentally left her room and closed the door behind me before walking back to my own. As soon as I took a step in the door, light blinded me. I blinked several times before realising I was looking through my own eyes. Also, that Alistair had grabbed me when I was leaving Toris' body and was now really close to my face. I flushed and pushed away from him.

"Well, I don't want to try going there again any time soon," I sighed. "No offence Tori. That was just too weird for me."

"It's fine," she laughed. "So we off to our next class?"

I shook my head, "No, I have a spare and I've been asked to stay here."

"Alright then. We'll see you at lunch," Chelsea said.

I nodded and they walked off, meeting up with the rest of the girls and leaving with everyone else.

"We're going to head to class too," William said. "We'll let you two spend some time alone."

He wiggled his eyebrows suggestively. I blushed and punched him in the arm. He rubbed the aching appendage.

"Hey, I was only kidding!"

Rolan rolled his eyes but there was a smile on his lips.

"Come on, idiot," Rolan sighed and dragged William away.

"Ta-ta," he called.

Aura and I started laughing. Aura hugged me then grabbed Mikais' hand.

"I'll see you at lunch, okay?" She asked.

I nodded and she waved, leading Mikai to their next class. Timothy came back from talking with Michelle, who was walking away with the other teachers. They *do* have classes to teach after all.

"Alright, are you ready to begin then?" Timothy asked, rubbing his hands together.

I raised an eyebrow and looked at Alistair who shrugged.

"Sure," I drawled.

-X-

"I'm not hearing anything," I muttered.

"Concentrate, Mary," Timothy pushed.

"What the hell do you think I'm doing? Peeling potatoes?" I snapped.

He sighed and pinched the bridge of his nose.

"Alistair, perhaps you could help her concentrate better," Timothy sighed. "I've got to go."

With that, he just left. I stared after him with a raised eyebrow.

"Well, that's a bit rude. He's the one that asked me to stay back in the first place."

Alistair took a seat directly across from me. We were alone now. I shifted uncomfortably at the thought.

"Close your eyes," he said.

I was reluctant but did so anyway.

"Now, don't think of anything."

"I've already tried that-"

"Then think of the voice," Alistair cut me off. "Think of when it has spoken to you and why."

I immediately thought of Bethany and what she meant to me.

'**She is a special person,**' the voice whispered.

'*She is,*' I answered before realising I had found the voice.

'**It's been a while, Mary.**'

Knowing exactly who she was, I noted that she sounded exactly like my younger self, just like she did back when I was five.

'*You actually left.*'

'**You were ignoring me. You didn't need me anymore.**'

I knew it had disappeared after that.

"-Mary," I tuned in to hear Alistair calling to me.

"Huh?" Was my intelligent reply.

He smirked and I turned my head away in embarrassment.

"You lost focus there for a second," he spoke. "Did you find it?"

I nodded. "Yeah. She's just like I remember," I told him.

"Ah," was all he said. "You and your inner voice had a strong connection back then."

"I guess we did. I was lonely as a child. She was with me everyday for two years before my caretaker told me to ignore her."

"You will get that bond back," he assured me. "In the meantime, work to keep that connection and talk to her. Find out how you truly see things."

I must have made a stupid face because he started chuckling at me. I blushed and looked away again.

"They are us and know exactly what we desire and despise. The sooner you realise how you truly feel, the faster you grow as a person," he explained.

"Oh," I drawled. "I think I know what you're talking about now."

"Good."

For the rest of my spare, I spent talking to my inner being.

'We're very strong, you and I,' she said.

'Really?' I asked.

'We inherited much from our father,' she said. *'That is why you need to be absolutely ready when we start merging.'*

'So what's new with you?' I laughed at the irony, purposely ignoring the strange look I was getting from Alistair.

-X-

I sighed in relief at the bell that rung.

"Finally!" I cried in joy.

I don't know if I was imagining it, but I could have sworn Alistair just smiled.

"Lunch time," I sighed thankfully.

I jumped up from my seated position, only to notice that Alistair had beaten me to standing. I raised an eyebrow. I guess I'm not as observant as I'd like to think.

'Or maybe you just do not notice because you were too busy thinking about his-'

'You're so perverted,' I scowled, blushing.

'I have no idea what you are talking about,' it stated. *'I was merely going to say that you cannot stop thinking about his abs. What do you think you were thinking about?'*

I blushed.

'And you call me perverted."

"-Mary?"

"What?" I asked, looking up into Alistair's eyes.

He merely smirked. I huffed and turned away.

"Whatever," I scowled. "I'm hungry," I stated before heading out of the gymnasium.

I met up with the girls in the courtyard.

"So how was Alistair?" Chelsea asked.

I rolled my eyes.

"Hardy ha-ha," I spoke, voice deadpan.

They laughed at my discomfort. What lovely friends.

"Did anyone bring any food for lunch?" Tori asked, looking at us and I could tell by the faces my friends made that no one thought to bring any food.

"Oh, I did!" Sera exclaimed happily.

"What did you bring?" I asked.

"Chicken and avocado sandwiches."

"How many did you bring?" Chelsea asked.

"I made six sandwiches because I knew you guys would forget," she said, sounding so proud of herself.

"Sera," I murmured slowly.

"Yes?"

"Have I ever told you that I love you?"

She giggled and handed us our lunch as we sat down.

"Hey guys!" We turned to see Aura with Mikai, Alistair, William and Rolan.

We all waved. Aura kissed Mikai on the cheek before running to us. The guys hung around the table we were at before, talking about god knows what.

"So how was Alistair?" Aura asked.

"Oh my god!" I shouted exasperatedly.

She gave me a weird look as my friends laughed.

"Did I miss something?" She asked.

"No, nothing at all apparently," Chelsea laughed.

She continued to look at us with a raised eyebrow. We went on munching on our sandwiches when I saw the girl again. She was staring at me.

I stared back. "Who is that?" I asked.

My friends turned to see who I was looking at.

Aura whistled. "Oh, tough luck," Aura stated. "That's Midnight. She's what the wolves call Nedorit," she explained. "It means 'unwanted' because not many wanted her in the pack. That's all I know."

I looked at her with a raised eyebrow.

"What did you mean by 'tough luck'?" Chelsea asked.

"Midnight doesn't seem to like you," Aura shrugged. "She's known to attack those she doesn't like."

"Why the hell would she attack me? I never did anything to her," I stated, frowning.

I turned back to Midnight. She was no longer staring, but glaring at me now. I glared back. I heard her growl deep in her throat and I responded with a hiss.

"You don't want to mess with her," I heard.

I broke eye contact with Midnight and turned to my left to see Leo, Jye, Blade and Kalum approaching.

"Hey guys," I greeted.

They each gave a wave. They stopped a few feet from us.

"What are you guys doing?" I asked.

"We were lying around when we saw Midnight tense up," Kalum explained.

"When we looked to see who her next unfortunate victim would be, we saw it was you," Leo stated.

"You don't want to mess with her," Jye repeated.

"What's her problem anyway?" I asked.

"We don't know. She just gets worked up sometimes," Blade said.

"Is she a part of your pack?" I asked.

"No. Her pack is smaller than ours," Leo stated.

"God, I'm starting to hate this school."

The bell went, signalling the end of period six and ultimately school for the day.

"Thank god school's over," I murmured.

"Home time now!" Bethany exclaimed.

We walked to mine and Sera's car. Before we got into any car, my phone rang.

"Yeah?" I answered.

"Has school ended?" Brenton asked.

"Yeah, why?" I asked.

"I need you to come back to the city."

"What is it?"

"I want you to check out something."

"Is it that bad?"

"Yeah."

I let out a breath before nodding. "Alright, I'll be there as soon as I can," I told him.

After he gave me the address, we ended the phone conversation. I looked to my girls. I saw that not far behind them was Aura and the guys.

"Something big has come up with Brenton," I explained as I jumped into my car, not bothering to open the door.

"What do you want us to do?" Tori asked.

"If I need your help, I'll give you a call. If I don't, I'll meet you at home," I finished and they nodded before I tore out of the school grounds and towards the city.

8

Set Up

I STOPPED THE CAR AT THE address that Brenton gave to me and saw it was probably the shadiest part of the city. I said nothing as I got out and walked to Brenton and a few of his men.

"You made it," Brenton stated as he turned his head towards me.

"Of course," I nodded. "What happened with that train case?"

"They had a fight and were hit by the train."

"Lovely."

He led me into an abandoned apartment block. Once in the first room, a gasp escaped me. In the centre of the room was a bloody carcass. Of what, I have no idea. Whatever it was though, I felt sympathy for the painful death I knew it endured.

"What do you think it is?" Brenton asked me.

I stepped closed to the lump of flesh. Upon closer inspection, I found fur on the ground, around us. The carcass was definitely flesh and blood with no fur on them whatsoever. I forcefully unfolded the flesh, which seemed to have been forced together, like making a ball out of play dough.

Once the carcass was set right, I could fully see the extent of the damage it took. Its arms and legs had been forcibly removed and there was a medium sized hole in its stomach where the intestines had poured out of.

"The fur suggests that they could have been attacked by a werewolf," Brenton said.

I shook my head. I dipped my fingers in the blood before sticking them in my mouth, tasting the blood.

"The victim was a werewolf. He's in his human form," I cleared up.

"You can tell by the blood?" Brenton asked.

I nodded. "Yeah. Every animal has a different taste. A vampire can usually tell them apart. This blood tastes like a human but holds werewolf components that I've been trained to identify," I said.

"Damn, I was close," Brenton cursed.

"It was a good guess though."

"So what attacked the transformer?"

I raised an eyebrow. "Transformer? Really?"

He shrugged with a smirk playing on his lips. "I just finished watching *Transformers 3*. Give me a break."

I laughed. "Sorry. I forget sometimes that you're still young."

He hummed in agreement. "Tell me about it."

"I just did."

He pulled a face at me and I laughed. "You're so funny, smartass."

"I'd rather be a smartass then a dumbass."

"Touché."

A man behind Brenton cleared his throat. Brenton turned to him and I looked back at the corpse.

"It's hard to tell what killed him," I admitted. "It could be a vampire, werewolf, fey, anything."

"So we just wait it out?" Brenton hissed.

"There's not much else we can do."

-X-

Images of the mangled body haunted my dreams. For some reason, so did a little girl. It's not weird for me to have meaningless dreams, no matter how many times I tried to make sense of them. But I knew this girl.

I met her in my younger years when I was around five years old, the same age I had my inner voice. I had just been taken in by Amelia and I still did not like to fight or indulge in my vampire instincts. I remember Amelia had left me behind a petrol station, where I had to wait for her to come back from her hunt. Being half human, I could live off normal food. Amelia could only survive so long on human food though.

I was waiting for her with a few bags of chips and a chocolate bar when I saw her. She was so dirty, covered in blood and grime. I had approached her carefully and offered her food. She snatched the chips from me and scoffed them down, shooting me distrusting looks as if I was going to attack or hurt her. I tried talking to her but she was mute. At least, I think she was because she never said a word.

Some teenagers had come around, looking for trouble and decided we were their next victims. I defended the girl as much as I could, but I was still injured and traumatized from my parent's death that I did not put up much of a fight and was beaten down easily. I had reopened the wounds on my left arm while I was at it.

When I went down, I saw the girl attack the teen that knocked me down. He scrambled away, confused as to how a small girl could overpower him. When she started growling and snarling at them threateningly, I realized she was a werewolf. Her eyes turned to slits angrily and the teens ran off.

When they left, the girl offered me her hand. Looking at her arm, she had an open gash running up her right forearm and there was one on her hand, going from the start of her index finger and diagonally across her palm.

I showed her my left arm which was bleeding because all of the wounds had been reopened. She took in my wounds as I took in hers and I felt a bond form between us. I may not have known what the girl went through, or even what her name was, but we had both experienced trauma one way or another. She understood me and what I felt and I knew she was thinking the same.

Without another thought, we had clasped each others hand, blood mixing with blood and the bond we had felt strengthened into something that could never be destroyed; not with time or death. She would be with me as I with her, even if we hadn't fully understood.

I wonder where she is, even to this day. I wonder if she's okay, or if she thinks of me. I hope that she found happiness and that she found friends like mine who would be there for her as mine have been for me.

~X~

"Mary, wake up!"

I shot up in my seat and looked up to stare into the very red face of Konan. *'Shit,'* I cursed inwardly.

"Stay after class," he said before walking off.

"Dick," I muttered under my breath.

He continued on with his lesson as I tried not to fall asleep. It's been two months since the first werewolf corpse showed up. Since then, there've been six others, one a week, all having faced a similar death as the first.

I looked over to Jye who had forced himself to stay with us during Ancient History. His light brown eyes had darkened to black from lack of sleep. He wouldn't look me in the eyes nor has he spoken to any of us since the first body was found.

I guess it's understandable since people he most likely knew were turning up dead. Hell, they could even be from his pack! He says that he's with us to protect me from the other vampires but my friends and I know it's all bullshit. We've proven that we can take care of ourselves to the school so we don't need protection, much less me. I think Jye and the other werewolves believe I'm the one killing off their kind, though I don't know why they suspect me. I haven't done anything to even seem suspicious.

I'm not fairing too well though. I'm dreading the next call I get from Brenton because I know it's to tell me they have another body. They may not be humans but they are still living beings; living beings that are currently being hunted down by something for reasons unknown. All we know is that they're being disembowelled while still alive and that their hearts are being ripped from their bodies.

I cursed softly to myself before I felt a light nudge. I looked at Alistair who sat silently next to me. His eyes searched mine for something. I smiled at him to show that I was okay but when his eyes narrowed at me, I knew he didn't believe it.

On a more positive note, Alistair and I have become more then acquaintances and more as friends. Though I admit, I'm falling for him. He's perfect, what more do I need to say?

The bell went and I sighed as everyone around me stood and filed out for second lunch since this was period five.

"We'll see you later, okay?" Tori spoke softly.

The girls knew how much this latest case was affecting me. While I worked this case, the girls received other jobs from Brenton so as to keep the money coming in. I nodded and both her and Chelsea left. As the last person left the room, Alistair spoke.

"Mary," I looked up at Alistair who was standing at my side.

Alistair smirked at me before he bent down and cupped my chin, bringing me closer. I didn't have enough time to gasp before his lips were on mine. My eyes flew open in shock as I stared into his smug gaze.

"That's enough of that," Konan commanded.

Alistair broke the one-sided kiss as he straightened. He smirked at me again before he turned and walked out of the room. I looked at the teacher who had turned his back to me and then to Jye who only stared at me warily. Only one thought ran through my head, drowning out all of my other thoughts of the deaths and mistrust.

What the *hell* was that!?

~X~

I grumbled as I walked out of the classroom.

"Who does he think he is, kissing me like that?" I growled.

Jye followed alongside me before he stopped.

"What is it?" I asked.

He looked a little pained by something but otherwise ignored it.

"I have to go to the bathroom," he said.

I raised an eyebrow at him before a thought occurred to me.

"Hey, you know what? So do I."

Before class, Jye, Leo, Kalum and Blade had given me their energy drinks. They said they felt sick after having so many cans beforehand, so I drank the rest of theirs and now I had to go.

"Where's the closest bathroom?" I asked.

"The one at the end of the Math block," he said.

I was about to say the one near the Language block since it was in my line of sight. Alright, something's going on. I followed him to the Math block before he stared at me. I fought the urge to call him out before I walked into the toilets. It was empty. I shook my head as I walked into one of the stalls. Maybe I was just becoming paranoid with all the tension.

Once done, I flushed the toilet when I froze. I suddenly felt like I wasn't alone. I opened the door and walked out of the stall to see Midnight. We regarded each other silently, the hairs on the back of my neck standing on end. I stepped passed her, to the taps and washed my hands. I saw in the corner of my eye, her nose twitch before her eyes filled with fury.

Next thing I knew, my back was up against the wall. Midnight's hand was wrapped around my throat and also happened to be keeping me off the ground. I gripped the hand choking me, struggling against her hold while fighting to still breathe.

"You smell of Dylan's blood!" She snarled.

Who?

She must be talking about the last body we found last night. He was a young one, probably about eleven. It pained me to see that and I know Brenton is blaming himself for not having found the killer yet.

Then I realized something. The wolf foursome set me up. They purposely gave me their drinks so that I'd have to go to the bathroom where Midnight would finish me off. That was why Jye stayed with me in Ancient History. That's why he brought me to these toilets instead of the Language block ones. That's why he looked so god damn *guilty*!

My eyes narrowed on Midnight in anger. I treasure friendships and I hate being stabbed in the back. I also hate being set up to die in a fucking toilet.

I gripped the arm that held me and kicked off the wall, forcing Midnight back into the wall behind her. Her eyes flashed dangerously before she swiped at me with her claws. She managed to snare my glove and rip it off before kicking me in the stomach. I smashed into the taps, breaking them and the mirror. I landed on shattered glass and broken parts of the taps. I winced as I moved to get up but Midnight kicked my side and the momentum turned me over to face the ground.

I slowly got onto my hands and knees as she aimed another kick at my exposed side before I grabbed her ankle and brought my elbow down on her shin, snapping it. She screamed before she pulled out a gun and aimed it at my head. My eyes widened in fear before I forced myself to move. I dodged the first bullet before I grabbed her wrist and twisted it. She whimpered and it fell out of her grip. She glared up at me before her eyes caught sight of my scarred arm and her eyes widened. I felt all pressure from her disappear and loosened my hold on her without letting her go.

"Your arm," she said before she looked into my eyes again.

I stared back at her in confusion before she moved her arm in front of me, my hand still wrapped around her wrist. That's when I saw it.

The diagonal scar going across her right palm from the start of her index finger.

9

Reunited

WE STARED AT EACH OTHER, not knowing what to say to one another. This girl, the one with blond hair and ice blue eyes, is the same girl I met all those years ago.

I let her wrist go but she grabbed my arm. Her left arm traced my scars. I looked her up and down, thinking of the little girl I had met when I noticed the damage I'd done to her leg. I tugged on my arm and she looked up at me. I nodded to her leg and she followed my eyes down to her injury.

I helped her sit down so that she was leaning against the wall. She let out a cry of pain when she bumped her leg. It was sticking out at a bad angle and needed to be put back into place.

"This is going to hurt," I warned as I sat on my knees next to her.

She nodded and closed her eyes.

"One," I said before I snapped it back into place.

She yelled out in agony before breaking off into pants. She turned her head to me and glared.

"What happened to two and three?" She yelled.

I didn't bother to do anything else since she heals quickly but the blow to my head might have given me a mild concussion, so we just sat there, staring.

"Why did you do it?" She asked as she turned her head away.

"I didn't," I answered.

She turned her head back to me with a scowl. "After everyone that was taken, you smelt of their blood," she stated.

"That's because I find their bodies," I said.

She looked at me confused. "You've seen their bodies?" She asked.

I nodded my reply.

"How?" She asked. "We've never seen their bodies. We follow their scent to a room that smells of their blood and death. The bodies are never there."

"You should be glad," I said grimly. "I smell like them because it's my job. My job is to protect the humans. I stop Ascuns from killing them," I explained.

"That doesn't explain why you're involved," she snapped.

"I'm involved in this because I want to be!" I exclaimed causing her to draw back in surprise. "The first body I saw, I thought it was someone with a vendetta against him and that things would stop," I said. "Then a body would turn up every week. I've seen the bodies and no one deserves that so I've made it my business to find whoever the fucker is that's murdering innocent wolves, even if that means seeing every mangled body."

Midnight stared at me. "You're weird."

"I know."

Midnight looked down at her leg and gently touched it. When she felt no pain, she added more pressure yet she still felt nothing so she stood.

"Is it all good now?" I asked.

"Yeah, all good," she said, smiling at me. "You?"

"I'll live...kind of."

Midnight rolled her eyes. "That's so cheesy."

She offered me her hand and I was hit with a sense of Déjà vu. She seemed to notice it too. I smiled back up at her and took her hand. Our bloody hands clasped together and our unbreakable bond washed over me.

I was too young to understand it back then but now I know how strong it truly is. With that knowledge came along her real name too.

Aimee.

-X-

As we walked out of the bathroom, I was met by Jye, Leo, Kalum and Blade. They all looked surprised to see me alive and moving. *Fucking bastards...*

"Let me talk to them," Aimee said.

I grunted in reply.

"Whatever," I snapped. "My friends are waiting for me. *True* friends."

I saw them all look away guiltily. I spat at the ground in front of them before heading to the table we usually sat at. My friends were waiting for me. Sera, Cassidy and Reign gasped and I looked down only to realise I was covered in blood from my earlier fight with Aimee.

I had completely forgotten about that. I touched my bottom lip to find Aimee had split it with one of her kicks. Damn, no wonder no one stood a chance against her.

"What happened? You look like shit," Chelsea stated.

"Chelsea," Cassidy scolded. "That was rude."

"What?" She asked innocently. "I'm just saying."

"Thanks, Chels," I muttered. "I love you, too."

"What happened?" Tori asked.

When I explained everything to them, they were pissed.

"Those sons of bitches," Chelsea raged.

"Calm down, Chelsea," Tori soothed. "If anyone's to be angry, it's Mary. She is the one they set up to kill after all."

"Yeah but still," Chelsea huffed.

"So Midnight's name is really Aimee? And she was your first friend?" Sera asked.

"Yeah," I answered. "But hey, don't worry, Sera. You're still my perfect little sister. Nothing will ever change that."

She gave me a bright smile as all traces of sadness disappeared from her features and her eyes were lit with that childlike innocence that we all loved about her.

"Mary," a voice called and I immediately recognised it as Aimee's.

We turned to see her and the boys. They looked like shit and I could see the self-loathing they held for themselves. Aimee walked to me but I kept my eyes on the guys. I vaguely registered the fact that we had drawn a crowd.

Then Jye got down on one knee and bowed his head to me. The other three looked at him in shock before Kalum followed. Then down went Blade and Leo.

"What are you doing?" I asked.

"Mary, we're so sorry for everything," Jye said.

"We were just doing what we believed would make our kind safe," Kalum said.

"Please," Blade pleaded.

"Forgive us," Leo finished.

I stared at each of them, kneeling before me. I have *no* idea what the hell was going on. I looked to Aimee who was equally surprised. She stepped forward so she was right next to me.

"They are willing to bond with you, to make you part of their pack."

"Is that even possible? What the hell did you tell them?"

She shrugged. Helpful.

"Well then, what do I do?"

"Well, you can accept them or you could reject their apologies and turn them away," she said.

Now that sounded harsh. I had seen Jyes' eyes before his head bowed to me and I saw how much this whole misunderstanding was eating away at him. The other three were no different but Jye was the one who had to personally deliver me to Aimee, to my expected death.

Upon hearing my thoughts and my decision, she gave me instructions on what to do. I ran a finger across my fang, cutting it open slightly and I heard the vampires around us take a deep breath. Tori and Chelsea stepped closer to me, ready in case anyone fancied a taste from its direct source. Leo and Kalum were the first to move. Blade followed but Jye only stared. I nodded and he moved forward slowly.

Leo was the first to be 'christened' with my blood. I made a small mark on his forehead with my bleeding finger, leaving a red line. Kalum and Blade were next. Jye was hesitant as he looked up at me.

"It's okay," I sighed and that seemed to be what he needed to hear before he was marked as well.

"We are bound," the four males acknowledged.

"They will answer your call should you try to reach them," Aimee stated. "But first, they must go tell their Alpha about this occurrence and for them, it may not be pretty."

-X-

"So you have some control over four of the hottest guys I have ever seen," Chelsea stated. "What are you going to do now?"

Thankfully school had finished and we were back at the hideout. The boys had decided to lay low for now before facing their Alpha. I kind of felt bad for them. On a positive note, Aimee decided to move in with us so she's currently setting up a room next to mine.

I snorted at her question. "Well, we all know what you would do with four hot males," I shot back.

Chelsea shrugged. "I won't deny it."

Tori slammed her fist on the table. "And here I thought you were my lesbian lover," Tori raged teasingly.

"So, I have to be honest," Aimee said as she came down the stairs. "This has got to be one of the coolest places I have ever seen," she complimented.

"Why, thank you," I bowed.

"Alright, who's hungry?" Cassidy asked as she walked to the oven and pulled out some pies.

She put the pies on plates and I saw her go to the fridge and pull out a blood bag. She stabbed the tube into one of the pies and filled it with blood then she did the same to another one. When she finished, she looked up at me.

"Did you want blood with yours?" She asked.

I shook my head and she put the bag back into the fridge before bringing the pies to us. Tori and Chelsea obviously got the blood mince pies and we got the normal ones. We all sat at the table and ate. Aimee was staring into space as she ate her pie.

"Aimee, what's up?" I asked.

The girls all turned to Aimee at my question.

"I was just thinking," she said. "If you get a call about another body, can I go with you?" She asked.

My first instinct was to say no but then I remembered that these were her people that were being slaughtered like cattle. I weighed the pros and the cons before sighing.

"Alright," I conceded. "But only because these are your people."

She nodded and continued to eat. Dinner was silent after that as we hoped the bastard killer was caught before another teen was mangled.

-X-

The moment I woke up on Wednesday, I knew the day was going to be shit. I had slept in and didn't have time to have breakfast. I walked downstairs to see everyone had just finished pancakes.

"Don't bother to wake me for breakfast guys," I spat sarcastically. "It's all good. *Really*."

Cassidy and Sera looked guilty.

"We thought you and Aimee wanted to sleep in after going to see Brenton last night," Sera murmured.

My eyes softened when looking at those two and I sighed. Brenton had called last night with another body and as promised, I took Aimee with me. This time, the wolf was a twelve year old girl. Aimee took it badly and went into a rage. I had to wrestle with her so that she would calm down. She was an emotional wreck last night. I told her I didn't want her getting upset like that again so I wasn't going to take her with me next time. She argued and locked herself away for the night. We all heard her cry herself to sleep and I heard her whimpers from the nightmares I knew would follow her to bed. I stayed with her while she slept and didn't get much sleep myself.

"I'm sorry," I spoke gently.

"No, don't apologise," Cassidy assured me. "You've put yourself under a lot of stress and we're all worried about you."

"That's no reason for me to lash out at you guys."

"We should be heading out now," Reign input.

"What about Aimee?" Sera asked.

"We'll let her sleep in," I decided.

They nodded and we got in the cars.

Upon walking into my form class with Chelsea and Tori, I spotted Aura with the guys. My eyes met with Alistair's. I fought the urge to blush as I thought about the kiss and he smirked knowingly at me. Bastard.

We took a seat by them and Tori started conversing with Rolan while Chelsea talked with Aura.

"So what happened between you and Ali?" William asked, snapping me out of thought.

I jumped slightly in my seat and he laughed at me. I punched him in the arm.

"Ow," he whined. "I was kidding," he said, rubbing his arm.

"I don't care and there's nothing going on between me and *Ali*," I huffed.

"Yeah, sure," he said, wiggling his eyebrows at me suggestively.

I held my fist up threateningly and he scooted back with his arms up in defence. The sudden change in facial expression was too comical that I started laughing, and I don't mean small giggles. It was a full blown maniac laugh. Perhaps it was the stress and pent up emotion because I felt something wet slide down my cheek.

I saw a look of concern wash over Williams' face before I realised it was a tear. Before I could stop, many more tear drops followed the first and soon I was struggling not to sob.

"Alright, up we go," William said as he grabbed my hand and stood, lifting me to my feet before we disappeared out the door using Haste, an ability all vampires have.

I heard Tori and Chelsea following closely behind when William stopped. I looked up to see the rest of my girls. Cassidy captured me in a hug and I couldn't help but cry even harder. My friends were here for me and I don't know what I would ever do without them.

10

Mind Bonding

I SAT WITH THE GIRLS' AND William. They were all joking while I remained in William's arms that wrapped around me protectively. He's taken on the role of my older brother over the past month. Something Tori said brought a smile to my face and I felt a bubble of laughter escape my lips. We hung out in the courtyard until the start of period one bell went.

We headed to Maths with our teacher Anna Orwell. We went to our usual seats when Anna entered.

"Good morning everyone," she greeted.

None of us answered back; for good reasons too. She has a very biased opinion on half-breeds. She's made my life harder the moment I stepped into her class.

"Great," I murmured. "Just what I wanted first thing in the morning."

My friends nodded. For once, I actually paid attention in Maths. I took notes and I guess it succeeded in distracting me. Only when I would raise my hand to answer an equation, she'd completely ignore me as if I wasn't even breathing the same air. Instead, she'd pick Angela, her treasured student.

I ground my teeth, baring my fangs, quietly hissing.

'Calm down, Mary,' Chelsea warned.

'I have enough shit to deal with,' I growled.

'Just relax,' Tori soothed. *'She's a bitch. We all know it.'*

So instead of listening to the teacher, I had a mental conversation with them.

"Mary," Ms Bitch called.

"What?" I asked, looking up at her.

She glared down at me in disgust. Yes, we all know you despise dhampirs. Bite me. Pun intended.

"Factorize this equation," she sneered.

I looked at the board.

$x^4 + 5x^3 + 2x^2 - 20x - 24.$

...

...What.

The.

Fuck?

I looked down at my book to see we were doing simple interest. Then I looked back to the board.

$\underline{x^4 + 5x^3 + 2x^2 - 20x - 24.}$

The damn thing was practically glaring at me. I looked back to Ms Bitch to see the smuggest look I had ever seen and I realised that I would have done anything to wipe that smirk off her face. Looking at Angela, she had the same shit-eating grin as the teacher.

So I stood. Looking at the board, I smirked and followed Mary's Guide 101. When in doubt, cheat. Walking to the board, I turned to trusty mathematician, Cassidy.

'Cassidy, I need your help,' I pleaded.

'What is it?' She asked.

I pulled her into my mind so she could see it through my eyes. Yup, that's right. Since first performing this on Tori, we all practiced and perfected the *Mind Bond*. We decided to call it that since it was better than Bethany's *Mind-y-thingamajig*. She was not surprised by our choice.

'I'm the nice one and even I think she's a bitch,' Cassidy stated.

'Right?'

'Here, can I borrow your body?'

'Go ahead.'

'Thanks.'

I literally sat back and watched with a front row view as Cassidy solved the equation within my body. When she was done, she gave me back the reins. I knew she was smiling at her work and I would be too.

$x^4 + 5x^3 + 2x^2 - 20x - 24.$

Let $P(x) = x^4 + 5x^3 + 2x^2 - 20x - 24.$

$P(1) = 1^4 + 5 \times 1^3 + 2 \times 1^2 - 20 \times 1 - 24 = -36$

$P(-1) = (-1)^4 + 5 \times (-1)^3 + 2 \times (-1)^2 - 20 \times (-1) - 24 = -6$

$P(2) = 2^4 + 5 \times 2^3 + 2 \times 2^2 - 20 \times 2 - 24 = 0$

$\underline{x^3 + 7x^2 + 16x + 12}$

$x - 2 \mid x^4 + 5x^3 + 2x^2 - 20x - 24$
$\underline{x^4 - 2x^3}$
$7x^3 + 2x^2$
$\underline{7x^3 - 14x^2}$
$16x^2 - 20x$
$\underline{16x^2 - 32x}$
$12x - 24$
$\underline{12x - 24}$
So $P(x) = (x - 2)(x^3 + 7x^2 + 16x + 12)$
Good *god*.

When I turned around to face the class, I tried to wipe the shocked look off my face. I mean it was 'me' that just worked out that equation. I saw the look the teacher and even Angela were giving me after 'I' had worked out the sum. I pulled the same shit-eating grin they wore before when they thought they had me.

Once Ms Bitch snapped out of her shock, she turned red.

"Mary, to the office!" She yelled.

My grin disappeared instantly. "For what?"

"Now!"

"Hold on a second," I spoke up. "Is it because I just embarrassed you in front of your class?"

"Mary, leave. Now!"

"I didn't do anything wro-"

"GET OUT YOU DISGUSTING HALF-BREED!" She screamed, causing a few of the students at the front of the classroom to jump.

"And the truth comes out," I spat, glaring at her angrily.

I stalked forward, backing her up against a wall.

"I may be a half-breed," I hissed, "but I have more honour and dignity then you self-righteous Spori."

I turned and headed to the door.

"Mr Rubyvale, make sure she makes it to the principal's office."

Angela's smirk fell. "Wait, Ms Orwell-"

"I don't want to hear another word," Anna strained. "Mr Rubyvale, if you would."

Alistair nodded and stood from his seat beside Angela and walked to me. His face remained emotionless but I saw the look in his eye. My eyes narrowed at him.

We exited the room and headed down the hall. The moment we turned a corner, he had me up against a wall and lips against mine as if his life depended on it. I didn't struggle but responded with just as much urgency. My arms wrapped around his neck and drew him closer as he pressed me against the wall with his body. He kissed down my neck and I gasped when his fangs sunk into my skin.

Pleasure blinded my vision as I arched into him. The feel of him drawing blood from me left me breathless.

'I really don't think you should be doing this in the hall,' the voice told me.

I didn't want to stop.

'Someone's coming,' it warned.

That caught my attention. Alistair noticed too because he pulled back and I dropped to my feet. In an instant, I had fixed my hair and clothes. Alistair had pulled my hair from its usual up-do. I didn't have enough time to fix it so I had just brushed my hands through it and just flicked it to one side. Alistair quickly leant down and licked my throat. I flushed before I realised he was just healing the bite mark on my neck.

I shivered involuntarily before he straightened. He watched me with a lust filled gaze and a smudge of my blood on his lips. He licked it away easily, smirking in the process before we kept walking just as the person turned the corner.

It was a teacher; Mr Wrath to be more specific. He looked at Alistair with a frown, then to me with a glare.

"What are you doing out of class and why does it smell like blood here?" He asked.

I clenched my right hand, cutting my palm before I held my hand out to him.

"I was causing trouble and was sent to the office. I got angry and cut myself accidentally," I stated.

He merely snorted. "Why am I not surprised?" He sneered. "Hurry up and make sure you get there."

Then he walked off.

"Prick," I hissed before we kept walking.

Alistair took my hand and licked it clean of my blood. I merely watched him. When did he steal my heart?

~X~

I had to spend the rest of the day in the office but luckily, Alistair was allowed to stay with me. Why he would want to, I have no idea but I wasn't about to complain. Whenever the teachers or principal left us alone, Alistair would continue what he started and I was more than happy to oblige. Is this love?

'You do love him,' my inner voice told me.

Once the bell for the end of school rang, we left. Alistair grabbed my hand in the middle of the hallway and I turned to him in surprise. He kissed me again, only this time it was gentle and sweet.

"I'll see you tomorrow," he murmured against my lips.

My knees felt weak from the intense feelings raging inside of me like a hurricane. I couldn't answer so I nodded instead and just left it at that. He smirked at me before releasing my hand and heading back the way we came.

I continued in the direction we had been heading in until I met with my friends in the car park.

"Why are you smiling like that?" Bethany asked.

"Oh my god, look at her lips," Sera pointed out.

I touched my lips. "What?" I asked. "What's wrong with my lips?"

"They're swollen," Tori pointed out.

"You've been making out with someone," Chelsea stated.

I blushed.

"It was Alistair, wasn't it?"

"Yeah, I have to meet up with Brenton now," I said offhandedly. "So I'll see you guys later."

I jumped in my car and took off, their laughter getting quieter with distance.

11.

TRUTH, LIES AND SAVING JYE

I T'S BEEN ABOUT FOUR WEEKS since the girls caught on to what was going
on between Alistair and me. Today, Thursday, I just knew it was going
to be another shit day. It started off alright when I had a good nights sleep
and felt refreshed in the morning. Then it got better when I had music first
up off the bat. I thought I was being paranoid. Then, period two came
along, which meant Math with Orwell. I was pissed before I even entered
her class.

Orwell just glared at me as I took my seat between Tiny and William.
Not only was the teacher constantly death glaring me, Tiny and William
were ignoring me, shooting me weird looks every now and then. I couldn't
understand what was going on. I also noticed Angela was sitting a lot closer to
Alistair then usual. That wasn't weird. The fact that he let her was. I shrugged
it off as just being paranoid again. After all, it's me he kisses.

Thinking about that made me smile and I managed to pass Math without
too much trouble. In English Literature though, it was exactly the same thing.
Angela was still sitting practically up against Alistair. Jealousy bubbled inside
me, I knew it. I wasn't going to deny it and because my seat was behind them,
I had a good seat to watch her bust a move on Alistair.

I grit my teeth and flexed my fingers. Looking down, I noticed my nails
had sharpened dangerously. The nails on my left hand poked out of my black
and purple striped glove.

"Shit," I cursed, retracting them.

I sighed and sat back, looking up at the ceiling. The things Alistair did
to my heart. He constantly breaks the composure I've spent years to perfect.
Within a few months, he brings me to my knees with a kiss. It's disgusting.

The lesson passed and it was lunch time. I walked out, talking to Tori and
Chelsea as we headed to our usual table. We stopped by the toilets for Tori

since she has this thing where she pees every forty-five minutes. As we got to the courtyard, we met up with the other girls.

"Hey, what are you guys doing?" I asked.

They looked forward and I followed their gaze to see Angela with the boys and Aura. Angela said something that made Aura lunge for her but Mikai grabbed her around the waist and held onto her. Angela smirked and flicked her hair before walking off with Alistair who followed behind her. We all watched in confusion. As we approached the others, Mikai, Rolan, William and Tiny shot me sympathetic looks while Aura threw her arms around me.

"I'm so sorry," she whispered.

What the hell?

"Sorry for what?"

She said nothing so I turned to Mikai who didn't look me in the eyes. I looked over to Rolan and William who were looking more uncomfortable by the second.

"Last night, we had a Vechi Adunare," William stated.

"What's that?" I asked.

"It means 'Ancient Gathering'," Sera clarified. "It's where the ancient families come together for a meeting to discuss the kingdom and whatnot. I was there."

"Okay," I drawled. "Go on."

"The two vampire families, Tare and Leal had revealed they plan to join together," William continued.

"Yeah. And?" I asked.

"To do so, they decided that the heir to the Tare and the heiress to the Leal would marry," Rolan explained.

"I think it's a wonderful idea," Sera said.

The guys and Aura looked at her.

"Never mind her, keep going," I urged.

"This had apparently been planned for a while between the two families, choosing last night to reveal it to the rest of us," Rolan continued.

"So what? Why would I care if the Tare and Leal married each other?" I asked.

"As you know, I'm from the Leal and Rolan's from the Tare," William stated. "What you don't know is that Angela is my cousin while Alistair is Rolan's."

It took me a second to register what they just told me. Alistair is from the Tare and Angela is from the Leal? Then it clicked. The colour drained from my face.

Alistair was getting married to Angela.

"Sera, why didn't you tell me?" I asked, turning to her.

She shook her head with wide eyes. "I didn't know!" She exclaimed. "I didn't know Alistair was a Tare. I'd never spoken to a member of the vampire family until last night. I didn't know Alistair's Vala was Ion Tare and he wasn't there last night so I didn't see him!"

"Most Ancients change their name to fit in with today's society," Rolan added. "My Vala is Virgil Tare."

"And mine's Felix Leal," William reintroduced.

"I'm so sorry, Mary," Sera spluttered.

I shook my head. I didn't want to hear it. If I had to hear any apologies, it was from Alistair himself or Ion or whatever the fuck he went by.

"How long ago had this been planned?" I asked icily.

"I believe the end of last year," Rolan told me.

I stood there, unsure of what to do. I felt multiple emotions running through me at that moment; anger, sorrow, pain, betrayal, humiliation. Just to name a few. I clenched my fists before looking up at them.

"I'll be back."

~X~

I found them inside one of the lab rooms, having a private conversation I guess. When I entered, Angela sneered at me while Alistair faced me with a look void of any emotion. No passion. No lust. No want. Nothing. That's all the confirmation I needed.

"Why?" I asked Alistair, staring at him.

"Why what?" Angela spat.

"Why did you do it?"

He said nothing as he stared down at me. He didn't make a sound or a move. It only angered me further.

"Why did you use me!?" I snapped at him. "I thought…"

No, I couldn't finish that last sentence. It was too humiliating to admit that I thought he liked me as much as I liked him. Tears were welling in my eyes but I didn't care. My heart ached from knowing it was all a lie.

"Why? Why *me?*"

I turned my head away from them as the tears fell. My hair, that I had chosen to leave down today for him, followed the movement and covered my face from their view like a curtain.

"How pathetic," Angela sneered. "You truly believed Alistair would actually like someone like you?" She asked. "We're True Born, and you are nothing but a hybrid!"

She laughed and I wanted nothing more than to tear her throat out with my teeth. The bell rang and she turned, flicking her hair.

"Come, Alistair," she insisted. "We have class."

She headed out of the room. Alistair stayed a moment longer before following her out and I was left to watch them leave. For the love of my life to just walk away.

I can honestly say that it was the first time I ever truly hated being a half-breed.

~X~

I skipped the rest of school, choosing to be alone at home. I don't know how long I was lying on my bed but it didn't feel too long before my friends joined me in my room.

"Mary?" Sera asked.

I didn't want to see them. Not when I looked this pathetic. I chose not to answer.

"We know you're awake," Chelsea sighed.

"Go away."

"What friends would we be if we left you on your own?" Tori asked.

"Friends that listen."

"Well, too bad we're your best friends," Cassidy said.

"That means we ignore everything you tell us in order for us to help you," Reign smiled.

I sat up and stared at them. Their eyes softened visibly.

"Your eyes are red," Bethany stated.

"Come on, let's go wash your face, babe," Tori suggested.

She grabbed my arm and guided me off the bed. To be honest, I felt like I was dead. Well, in a way, I'm half dead but that's not what I mean. After months of affection, I couldn't help but fall in love. No one else had ever shown me such attention. The only male attention I had before Alistair was either that of my father or when the enemy wanted to drain me of all my blood. I guess I had become dependent on Alistair's attention. He made me feel alive again and I haven't felt that way since my parents were taken from me. Now that that's all over, I don't know what I'm going to do.

I did as the girls wanted but I didn't feel any better. I don't know if I ever will.

-X-

It's been a few weeks. I was practically useless now. I didn't go to school because I didn't want to face Alistair and *Angela*. Her name made me sick to my stomach and my blood calling for her death. I haven't been eating or sleeping. Looking in the mirror, I have become paler and my eyes darker. There were bags under my eyes from lack of sleep. Hurray, Mary. You're depressed.

"Mary!" Sera called.

My head shot up when I was suddenly hit by the smell of blood. My eyes flashed crimson as I inhaled the sweet, copper scent. So delicious. I raced downstairs and found myself before Kalum. He was badly injured from what looked like a fight. The lights that lit up the kitchen showed me his blood seeping into the carpet. A cough splattered blood onto my face and thoughts of drinking him dry crossed my mind before I realised what it was I had been thinking. I grit my teeth in anger.

I was *not* a monster! Well, I am but—

"What happened?" I asked.

He finished his coughing fit before speaking.

"Our Alpha came to us when he sensed that something had changed within the pack. We spent these past weeks trying to come up with a way to talk to him that we didn't even realise we hadn't seen the pack for a while and he had come looking for us."

"Where are the others?" I asked.

He looked down. "We were taken by surprise when he showed up at our apartment and when he smelt your scent on us from being bound to you, he attacked. Jye went down first being too slow to react and he was standing right by him. Blade and Leo put up a fight but he is still our alpha and so their heart wasn't in it and they went down next. When he turned to me, I tried to plead your case. It earned me a good beating but instead of knocking me out like the others, he told me to prove that you are worthy of being part of our pack through us," Kalum murmured.

Anger washed over me like a heatwave. All the suffering I had endured over the past weeks fuelled my rage and this blatant abuse of my friends was the final straw.

Sera gasped and stepped away from me. Instantly, I knew my eyes were glowing brighter and quickly diverted my gaze.

"Mary, you need to calm down," Cassidy soothed.

"I say we kill them," Reign suggested.

Cassidy glared at her. "Not helping."

I called for Aimee as Reign and Sera healed Kalum. Within a few minutes, Aimee was by my side. When she saw Kalum, I could tell by the narrowing of her eyes that she understood the situation.

"The Alpha?" She asked.

I nodded and she clenched her fists.

"What are we going to do?" Bethany asked.

"Mary needs to face him," Aimee replied. "If she doesn't face him, he could order the boys to break the bond with her."

She addressed Kalum with a look of approval. "Defending Mary and your bond with her saved the bond you share."

-X-

Running beside him, Kalum led the way for us. Beside me, Aimee kept. She was a beautiful silver wolf with glowing azure eyes. Her fur had a blue tint to it and shined mystically.

He led us outside of town and into the bush that surrounded Alexandra Hills. The longer we ran, the angrier I became. Soon, we slowed and stopped in a small clearing. I looked around, scanning the darkened brush. I could smell my three wolves and feel them so clearly, it was almost like a physical pull. As I came to a stop beside Kalum, Aimee joined me and both wolves transformed back.

"Mary," a voice groaned.

I turned to see Jye on his knees facing me about fifty metres from where we stood and beside him were Leo and Blade. What caught my eye though, was the male standing behind them.

"Maven," Kalum spoke.

He looked to be in his late twenties. He had light brown hair that ruffled in the breeze and piercing blue eyes that seemed to try and turn my blood to ice. If I hadn't been through what I had, it may have worked. I saw Kalum tense just slightly. From the darkened brush to Maven's left stepped out a female with long strawberry blonde hair. Her stance was strong and confident, border lining cocky. She must be his Luna. On his right stepped out another male. I'm assuming he was the Beta wolf. Around us, pairs of eyes glared from the shadows.

"You must be the one they tied themselves to," the man spoke.

He then turned to Kalum.

"You spoke the truth? I half wish you had lied to me," he snapped.

He glared down at the three wolves bowed before him.

"You are a disgrace to our kind!"

He kicked Jye harshly in the back, forcing him to plummet forward, face first into the dirt.

"Let them go," I hissed.

"Wait," was all Aimee said and I grit my teeth before nodding slightly.

"Ah, if it isn't the infamous Midnight," Maven spoke carelessly but the sneer on his face directed towards Aimee wasn't nearly as forgiving as the tone of his voice before continuing. "Not only did they fail to kill you, Vampire, but they made you part of the pack without my permission."

"I'm here to prove myself," I spoke up.

"Do you know what that entails?" Maven asked. "I have to admit that I am surprised that a bloodsucker cares so much about those born of the moon's curse."

I snorted. "I'm a hybrid, I have no reason to be biased."

The man chuckled gruffly. "No, I suppose not. Then again, wolves don't hold such resentment towards hybrids."

"Just vampires," I stated flatly.

"Why so bitter? It's ancient old news that vampires and werewolves are mortal enemies. Even the humans know that."

I cast a fond look towards Aimee and she shared my moment of reflection before offering me a nod before a small smile of support.

"Times are changing," I merely replied, most of the anger lifting.

It wasn't his fault. It was tradition. Routine. And there were rules that you had to follow that the boys didn't. My eyes skipped to the people that had stepped out of the brush to form a type of circle around Maven, only it didn't close. It was open, daring me to enter.

As I walked forward, I could feel Kalum's concern.

"You will prove your worth fighting my Beta, Chuck."

The circle closed behind me and I watched as the well-toned male stepped out of the circle formation to stand between Maven and I.

I watched him warily and for once, I was thankful that my opponent had no smirk or sneer but was looking at me warily in anticipation. As I opened my mouth to speak again, I almost doubled over when my throat and chest was assaulted with a burning sensation. A hand flew to my throat as tears stung my eyes.

Out of the corner of my eye, I saw Aimee had actually recoiled.

The distraction could not have come at a worse time because Chuck didn't wait for me to recover as he lunged. With the thirst burning my throat, my concentration was scattered and my strength weakened.

I took punch after punch, kick after kick and scratch after scratch.

"Surely you can do better than this," Maven called after I was thrown to the other side of the circle.

I rolled a couple of metres before coming to a stop. I dug my nails into the dirt, my body screaming at me in pain. I managed to lift my head up to see Maven's boots by my head. Raising my gaze, I made eye contact with him.

"Ah, I see," he murmured. "You have not fed in a while."

"You may as well stay down, Vampire," Chuck called.

He wasn't taunting, merely stating the best course of action to take.

I shook my head and pushed myself up but the moment I was upright, I was kicked back, soaring into a tree. The tree cracked -or maybe it was my back- as I dropped onto the roots, breaking a rib or two from the fall.

Chuck walked towards me. I struggled to raise myself onto all fours.

"Stay down."

I spat blood onto the grass before me. I managed to see the tensing of Chuck's leg, the tell tale sign of an incoming kick. With the last of my strength, I caught his leg and drove my elbow into the side of his kneecap, snapping it. Chuck howled in pain while I collapsed, panting.

Chuck fell on his ass, unwilling to put any pressure or move his broken leg.

"Alright, I've seen enough," Maven announced, ending the Proving.

I forced my body to get up, fighting off the nausea and head-spin.

"You are at your weakest and have not fed in what seems to be quite a while. Why would you come here, knowing you have little strength and practically defenceless?"

I stumbled on my feet, mentally noting my left ankle was sprained as I wiped the blood that had dripped down my chin.

"Because they needed me," I slurred.

A concussion too.

"Your performance was pathetic and left much to be desired. But your will and loyalty made up for it. The bond may remain."

As if he said the magic word, my legs gave out and fell. Thankfully, Aimee was there.

"I've got you, don't worry," she spoke soothingly.

Even though I wanted to cry, vomit and scream from the stress my body just went through, I managed to crack a smile.

"Let's go home," I wheezed.

12

Study Break Over

"I can't believe I let you guys drag me here," I muttered.

We stood before the high school. I hadn't been here since Alistair's painful betrayal. My friends thought it would be good for me to come back after I got most of my anger and other negative emotions out with the fight against Maven.

"I still think you should have killed him," Reign put in.

"Reign!" Cassidy snapped sternly.

"It's Monday. A new week, which means a new start," Reign changed the subject in a sophisticated tone.

I rolled my eyes. Today, I wore black jeans and a white shirt with a small black hooded vest over the top and my trusty black glove on my left arm.

The bell rang, signalling the start of school. I sighed.

"Let's get this over with," I groaned.

-X-

Since today was Monday, that meant that first up, I had Music. I slouched a bit. That also meant I'll see Alistair and Angela. *Together.* I may have come to terms with it but that doesn't mean I have moved on *or* okay with it.

"I hate being the bigger person," I grumbled.

The girls shot me sympathetic looks.

"At least you have Aura in that class," Cassidy argued.

I had forgotten. Aura had changed from Art with Mikai, Cassidy, Reign and Bethany to be with me in Music. She's such a caring friend.

"Yeah, you're right."

I headed to my class the long way by walking the girls to their classes. By the time I reached the music room, I was about fifteen minutes late. I stood outside the classroom, staring at the door. I reached up to knock then hesitated.

Why did you use me!?

Flashes of that day haunted me as my words echoed around in my head, threatening to cast me back into the black depths of depression. I took a step away from the door.

'I thought you liked me back…' I thought sadly, eyes dropping.

'*Cut it out,*' my inner voice yelled. **'*You're better than that. You did not spend those two weeks locked in your room for nothing. You can't let yourself go back to that otherwise you really are nothing but a pathetic half-breed.*'**

My eyes narrowed. She was right. She's absolutely right. I won't let myself go through that again and I won't give Angela the satisfaction of seeing me waste away.

With the temporary confidence, I knocked on the door. It wasn't long before Michelle answered. Her eyes widened when she saw me.

"Oh, Mary! You're back," she declared.

The noise inside the classroom came to a stop and I knew they were listening.

"Welcome back," she smiled at me as a mother would her child.

I smiled back and entered. Every pair of eyes was on me.

"Mary!" Aura exclaimed before tackling me in a hug.

I grunted when she almost knocked me down. I awkwardly patted her back.

"Hey Aura," I wheezed. "Can you loosen up a bit? It's hard to breathe with you squeezing the life out of me."

She laughed sheepishly before releasing me. "Heh, sorry."

"No problem."

"Alright class," Michelle announced. "It's time to start practicing your songs."

The class did as they were asked and began to file out the doors that led to the sound proof room. Soon it was just Aura and I left in the class room. I followed her to her violin that lay forgotten near the piano.

"How about a duet?" She asked.

My eyes widened and I shook my head furiously.

"I'm getting better but I'm not *that* good," I sputtered.

Aura shrugged. "So? You've got to start somewhere."

"No."

"Please?"

"No, Aura."

"Pretty please with a cherry on top?"

I rolled my eyes and sighed.

"Fine. What song?" I asked.

She pulled piano sheet music out of nowhere before handing it to me. I stared at her for a bit. I read the title. *My Heart Will Go On*. Really? I looked at Aura with a raised eyebrow.

"It's a beautiful song and I like it. Sue me," she laughed. "I'll let you practice. I'll be back later."

Then she left. I shook my head in disbelief before walking to the piano. I pulled my purple Billabong bag off my back and rummaged through it until I pulled out a lead pencil. Going through the music, I wrote in the notes before I started practicing. It wasn't long before I got the gist of it. When I was able to play the song all the way through, a smile broke out on my face. The sound of clapping drew my attention away from the piano keys.

My eyes narrowed. "What do you want?" I snapped.

Alistair's hand ceased their motion before just staring at me.

"You're getting better."

"Don't patronize me."

"No, really. You have improved since you first started here," he said, walking towards me.

"Stop where you are," I spat, glaring at him. "Just because we're making small talk doesn't mean we're friends. Stay the hell away from me."

He merely stayed where he was. I turned back to the piano, not really looking at it though. My vision began to blur from my tears.

"Leave me alone," I whispered brokenly.

A lone tear landed on the C key.

"I'm sorry."

I spun my head around so fast, I think I got whip lash. I glared at Alistair, willing him to combust into flames.

"Don't you dare!" I yelled. "Don't you dare apologise to me now! You didn't have the balls to apologise to me when I needed to hear it the most and for that, I'll never forgive you. I should have known you *True Born* were all the same."

"I think it's time you left, Alistair."

We turned to Aura who just entered. She stared at Alistair with a stony look on her face. Alistair nodded to her before he went back into the sound proof room.

"Are you okay?" Aura asked.

I nodded and wiped my eyes. "Yeah," I sniffed.

"Okay," she murmured before smiling brightly. "Ready for that duet?"

Next period was Konan Wrath's class and I can honestly say I was looking forward to it. No, I'm not losing it. I just know that Wrath will provide me with a distraction. Hey, who knows? Maybe I'll even do some work.

'Not likely,' my inner voice snorted.

'Shut up, you.'

'I am you so technically you are telling yourself to shut up.'

'Stop messing with my head. I'm going to get a headache soon.'

She was wrong. Today, Wrath was telling the story of Senina and Audrea, the first vampires to ever walk the earth. The reason why I was so interested in this story was because my dad would always tell me the story since I was named after Senina.

My dad named me Senina Anata Amare. That was my name, the name on my birth certificate but my dad told me there were people after him and that it was dangerous for me to go by that name. So my mom gave me a human name, Mary Hazel. Only in private and when he wasn't paying attention, would my dad call me Senina. If my mom was present at such times, she'd smack the back of his head.

While I can say I am Mary, I miss being called by my Vala. But regardless of my longing to hear my true name from my dad's lips, I respected his wishes by never revealing it. Not even my friends know about my Vala, perhaps Aimee does if she is able to dive that far into my mind with our special bond but no one else. So I take a little pleasure in hearing the story about Senina and Audrea.

I smiled to myself at the feeling in my stomach. Wrath may not be my dad and he may not be telling the censored version my dad did...

...But I felt like a child again.

~X~

After Vampire Studies, it was lunch and I was sitting at our table. I saw that Alistair no longer sat with them because Angela insisted that he stay by her side.

"I pity him actually," William stated, staring at the table Alistair now sat at with Angela and her flunkies.

"Tare are the second in command of the Draconis, meaning they are harsh in raising their young," Rolan continued. "Because Alistair is the heir of the Tare, he is under the constant watch of our elders and his father."

"He's right," Sera spoke.

We all turned to her.

"Being an heiress myself, I understand the pressure and expectations he must always exceed in order to appease his clan, his family."

Well, when she puts it like that, she makes me feel bad for Alistair.

"So what do you want us to do about it?" Chelsea snapped.

"Nothing. Just understand that he has always listened to his fathers' demands and does what his kin ask of him. I don't believe there was ever a day when Alistair did something for himself," Rolan finished off.

"That doesn't excuse the fact that he used Mary," Tori stated. "He could have been mind-controlled and I still wouldn't forgive him for what he did to her."

"Tori—" I started but she wouldn't listen.

"No, Mary. They weren't there when you fell into depression," she growled. "They didn't watch you starve yourself almost to the point of death. They didn't feel the helplessness we felt, knowing everything we tried to do to make you feel better wasn't working and fearing that you'd become a monster like the ones we fight. They don't understand what we went through. They may hold sympathy for Alistair and I agree; it is tragic that he doesn't have any freedom but he didn't have to lead you on like that. He was to marry Angela and he knew that, yet he chose that time to be selfish and ended up hurting you far worse than he could imagine. So if you guys want to defend him, by all means do so. That's your choice and I won't hold it against you, but if he wants my forgiveness, he's going to have to get on his knees and beg me for it and do a lot of ass kissing and that's just me."

Everyone was silent but from the look on Chelsea and Bethany's faces, they felt the same way.

I felt shock and guilt flood my veins. "Tori," I breathed out shakily. "I-I had no idea—"

"It's okay," she eased. "We know it wasn't your fault. You were head over heels in love with him and then you found out he was engaged. We can't begin to imagine how much that must have hurt you."

I didn't know what else to say. What *could* I say to that?

-X-

I sat with William as Rolan partnered up with Alistair for HPE. We were supposed to be conversing with our inner voices but William and I were arm wrestling.

"That's three - one to me," William gloated, lying on his stomach.

I rested in a similar position. "Shut up."

"Is someone a sore loser?" William teased.

'Show him whose boss.'

She didn't have to tell me twice. Fire flooded my veins but not in an unpleasant way. I gasped in surprise before my hand slammed William's down. I threw myself backwards in shock, ripping my hand away from his. Not only did his arm touch the ground, it ruined the wooden flooring, making it all uneven.

"Mary," William grunted in pain.

I looked down at him in fear. Not of him but of myself.

"I'm sorry," I whispered.

"It's okay."

"I could have broken your arm."

"Oh, please. You could have broken my arm without that power surge. That was...incredible," he said in awe. "Before you slammed my arm down, I felt the power through our linked hands. It was so...*raw*. You connected with your inner for just a moment. Most of us don't reach that stage until later on in our life."

I was still staring at the wooden crater.

"Do you think you could do it again?"

Now that caught my attention. I looked at him with disbelief.

"You...want me to...do that? *Again?*" I asked.

He nodded. "Yeah. Only this time, just let it flow between us instead of attacking me."

I shook my head. "I-I don't know if I can, let alone *want* to."

"Is everything alright?"

We both turned to see Timothy standing over us, eyeing the hole.

"Sir, is it possible to share power with someone else?" William asked.

I looked at him in shock. What was he *doing*? Did he *want* me to get in trouble? Timothy looked at him in confusion.

"Define 'share'."

"Well, you see Mary and I were having an arm wrestle. Before she slammed my hand into the ground, I felt her power through our hands."

"Oh yeah, sure. Just tell him everything that happened. Don't ask me if it's alright if he knows. Go ahead," I spat.

William shot me a smile that would melt even the toughest of females. It angered me more that it was working on me. Damn him!

"How interesting," Timothy murmured.

"I wanted to know if it was possible for her to share her power with me or something similar."

"Yes, I believe it is possible. There have been stories where vampires have shared their power to defeat a foe," Timothy stated. "It requires intense concentration and control otherwise the consequences could be fatal."

"..."

"Let's do it, Mary."

13

SENINA

M Y MOUTH HUNG WIDE OPEN as I stared at William.

"Are you joking?" I asked. "He just said that the consequences could be fatal and you still want to practice this?" I was almost yelling.

"Sure. As someone once told me, 'to not take risks is the biggest risk of all'," he said with a British accent.

"You can't be serious. You want to endanger your life because you want to *take a risk*?"

"When you say it like that, you make me sound stupid."

"You *are* stupid!"

"Well, that's not very nice."

"Oh my god, you're unbelievable."

"Thank you."

I fumed inwardly. God, he can be so frustrating!

"Look," he started. "Do it, just this once, with me. If it doesn't work, then at least we found out. It doesn't even have to have a big effect. I just want to feel that power again."

"If I say yes, will you drop it?" I asked.

He perked up. "Absolutely."

"Fine."

I sat back down and he moved from his lying position to a meditative one. I rolled my eyes. He wasn't taking this seriously. He could potentially die and he's fucking around. He took my hands and we closed our eyes.

I don't know what I'm supposed to do.

'That's where I come in,' my inner voice spoke up.

'What am I supposed to do?'

'Focus on your stomach, your core,' she instructed.

I did as she asked. I took a few deep breaths and cleared my mind before entering a meditative state. Going deep into my subconsciousness, I found it. My core in the form of a flame. It was purple in colour and intense in heat.

"This is me?" I asked.

Beside me, another version of myself appeared, only she was the five year old me. Her hair was longer, down to her waist and her eyes were bright red, surprisingly intimidating. On her forehead was an amethyst jewel in the shape of a diamond, much like my Dad's ruby triangle.

"Who...are..."

"I am the voice," she stated. *"Call me Senina."*

Her eyes held wisdom way beyond her years, perhaps even mine.

"Senina?" I asked.

"Because I am your pure-blooded half, it is only right that I go by our Vala," she explained.

I traced the jewel on her forehead.

"Makes sense."

I turned back to the large flame.

"This is my power?" I asked again.

She nodded. *"It is. This represents your current power level. If you concentrate, you can actually feel the flame getting hotter.'*

I closed my eyes and focused on the flame. It took a while but I did feel it pushing outwards slowly but surely.

"What does it mean?"

"You get stronger every day. Every Furiata does until they finally merge with their inner."

"What did you call me?"

"Furiata. It means 'Maddened'. A name given to those who harboured an inner being by those that don't understand."

"How do you know all this?" I asked. "If you're me, how do you know this when I don't?"

"This is all ancient knowledge which is passed down from generation to generation. Every True Born is born with the knowledge of their previous ancestors regarding vampires."

"Let me guess, I won't know what my dad should have passed down to me until I merge with you?" I asked.

"Precisely."

"Great," I muttered.

"Did you not come here for a reason?" She reminded me.

"Oh, right. I completely forgot. How do I connect with William the way he wants me to?" I asked.

She looked a little troubled for a second. *"I must insist that you do not go through with what he wants,"* she spoke. *"I'm afraid you're not ready to face the full extent of your powers, let alone* share *it* with someone.*"

"I know, Senina, but you know William won't drop this until I do."

"Yes, I do *know. Very well,"* she sighed. *"All you have to do is step into the flame."*

I looked at the fire that had increased in temperature since the last time I looked at it. She must be joking.

"I can assure you, I am not."

I turned so that I was facing the fire directly.

"Hey, Senina?" I called, not turning away from the fire.

"Yes?"

"Thanks for the help. I—" I paused for a moment before looking at her. "I can't wait to merge with you."

I couldn't see her and neither did she speak but I got the feeling she was smiling at me. I ran at the fire, closing my eyes.

-X-

I couldn't breathe. I couldn't see. I couldn't hear. What I could do though, was feel like I had molten lava coursing through my veins and not in the good way. I was screaming but no sound was coming out. There was just too much pressure and I felt as if I was going to combust. Then I felt something on my arm. It was cold and soothing, empty of whatever was filling me. I looked at where my arm should have been but it was void of anything. There was nothing to see. More power flooded my veins and I knew I was going to burst from the inside out so I did the only thing I could. Feed it into the empty, cold space attached to my arm. As more and more power flowed from me into the empty space, I felt as if the lava in my body was cooling in temperature while the space started to fill. Like a hot-air balloon, it started to rise and leave me. I knew that if I let it go, I was as good as dead. So I grabbed onto it and kept feeding more power into it until I felt it was going to burst but who cares? It's just a balloon.

'Let go, Mary.'

No. If I do, I'll die!

More and more power left my body and I felt as if the balloon was on the verge of exploding.

'Mary, let go.'

Didn't you hear me? I'll die if I let go! I'm almost finished-

'Mary, you're going to kill him! Let go!'

My eyes widened and I released my hold on the balloon. The dark abyss started to lighten to charcoal grey. My eyes darted around frantically, trying to give shape to anything near me. Slowly, I became aware of screaming.

'Mary, can you hear me?'

It was Sera.

'W-What's going on?'

I felt as if I had been hit by a train times ten. I didn't have the energy to do anything and my body burned as a lingering reminder of the previous power overload. The screaming from before became louder as my hearing caught up with the rest of my senses.

'Who's screaming?'

I fought against my body's wishes to remain lying down and forced myself to sit up. When did I even lie down? My eyes took in more light as I looked around. Everyone had gathered around us, forming a circle. Were they going to try to hurt me like last time? More screaming drew my attention to the sight before me and my eyes widened.

The person screaming was William. He had severe burns running up his right arm. His eyes were glowing red and unseeing and he just kept screaming. Rolan and Tiny were holding him down but that didn't mute his screams of pain. They were so loud and pain-filled that it brought tears to my eyes.

"What's happening to him?" I asked but it was ignored.

Teachers were yelling at the students to keep away or for help.

"You have to do something, Mary!" Sera yelled over the noise.

"Me? What can I do?!" I yelled back.

"How the hell should we know!?" Chelsea growled. "You're the one that did that to him in the first place!"

What?

I turned back to William who had tears falling from all the pain and I remembered Senina calling out to me.

Mary, you're going to kill him! Let go!

Oh my god, I did this to him. I struggled to my hands and knees and I knew there was no way I would be able to stand so instead, I crawled. I crawled to William who was still screaming bloody murder.

"Mary, get away!" Timothy yelled at me but I ignored him.

"Move!" I yelled at Rolan, who was straddling William's legs.

He said nothing but stood and backed up so he was holding down his ankles. I took his place and straddled William's waist.

'Senina, help me!' I pleaded.

I knew tears were falling now. You would be crying too if you were killing one of your friends from the inside out.

'Senina, please!'

I was desperate now. I'd do anything to silence William's screams.

'Bite him and leave it all to me!'

Normally, I would argue and question her commands but now wasn't the time. I trusted her so I did. In an instant, I swooped down and latched my teeth onto his neck and found myself lost in my subconsciousness again.

-X-

I stood before Senina, inside my flame.

I was still in it?

I looked down to see William trying to crawl away from me and the fire but something held him half in. Because it was increasing, his body was being engulfed in flames bit by bit. I went to help him.

"Don't touch him!" Senina yelled.

"Are you serious? He needs me!"

"If you touch him, he will become fully engulfed by the flame and end him where he lies," she told me.

I tried to step away but found I couldn't leave the fire. I looked at her, begging her for help.

"Then what do I do?" I asked.

"Leave it to me," she stated.

She walked towards us but stopped just out of William's reach.

"Mary!" He screamed, flopping onto his back.

His eyes showed so much anguish that I broke into sobs. He didn't even notice Senina.

"Help me!" He pleaded.

Senina closed her eyes and I looked up to see the top of the flame slowly tilting towards her before it was actually touching. Then I realised she wasn't touching it, she was sucking it in. Bit by bit, the flames that licked at William's lower half receded but I was losing strength, energy. I collapsed to my knees, barely able to stay standing. After a long and gruelling time, William was finally free of the fire. Senina reached in and pulled me out. I stumbled forward before losing all consciousness.

14

THE BALL

I GROANED AS I CAME AROUND to reality. I looked around to see I was in the school infirmary. Then the memory of what I had done flashed before my eyes. I cried softly, shaking as sobs racked my body.

"Mary?" A voice asked.

I turned to see William on the bed next to mine. How did I not see him?

"I'm sorry," I choked out.

"Hey, don't cry," he soothed.

"You almost died."

"Yeah I did, but that wasn't your fault," he tried to reason. "I was the one who pestered you to do it. Neither of us knew what would happen."

"But-"

"And the last time I checked, it was you who saved my life," he added. "I don't know what you did in there, but I made it out alive and only with burns, nothing else."

I didn't know what else I could say.

"I'll tell you what though, I don't want to be your enemy when you finally merge with your inner vampire," he joked.

I rolled my eyes and threw my pillow at him. He only laughed and tucked it nicely under his head.

"Seriously though, your power was so raw and dangerous that if I wasn't being fried to death, I'd have been high on adrenaline from being so close to death. It was...unforgettable."

"I don't know if I want to merge with Se- my inner vampire," I corrected.

"You were going to tell me your Vala, weren't you?" William perked, sitting up.

I frowned. "No."

"Don't lie. Come on, tell me!" He was almost bouncing in his bed. How was he even able to move after everything he went through?

'You have been in the infirmary for four days,' Senina informed me.

'What?'

"Come on, Mary!" William whined. "I told you mine!"

I rolled my eyes. "Fine, but you can't laugh, okay?"

"Why would I laugh?" He asked.

I shrugged. "Okay, my dad named me Senina Anata Amare. That's my true name."

William stared at me with wide eyes. "Amare?" He asked.

I nodded. "Yeah but my dad was hiding so Amare is a fake name he took on."

"What was his name?"

"Dragomir V. Amare."

He stared at me in silence with this strange look on his face.

"William?" I asked meekly.

He shook himself out of his daydream. "What?"

"Why were you looking at me like that?" I asked.

"I—" He thought for a moment. "I was just surprised. You were named after *the* Senina," he said. "You have quite the expectations to fill if you ever told anyone else your name."

"Well then, it's a good thing I wasn't planning on telling anyone else," I huffed. "You're the only one I've told my Vala to. You should feel honoured."

"Trust me, I do."

There was that look again.

"Cut it out!"

Another pillow followed the first.

-X-

Finally, we were released on the fifth day. Things were back to normal and this whole event was behind us. Because we were released on Saturday, no one was around. I didn't know why they kept us in there for so long. William said that the teachers don't have much of a life so they hang out at the school on holidays. To be honest, I believed him. I can't really see teachers having a life outside of school.

Rolan came around to pick up William and ended up giving me a lift as well. William ran to the car and opened the door for me.

"There you are, milady."

91

I rolled my eyes. "William, you've been calling me that since we woke up. Did you hit your head *that* badly?"

"Hey, I resent that," he pouted. "I haven't bumped my head since my mom dropped me when I was four."

Rolan tried to hide his smile as he silently laughed while I didn't bother to hide my mirth. I outright laughed at him as I was climbing into the back of the car. Rolan owned a dark red, cobalt Chevy. I loved the look and feel of it.

"Where can I get one of these?" I asked.

Rolan shrugged. "I don't know. My dad got me this."

"Favouritism," William whistled.

Rolan just looked at him. "You know I'm an only child."

"What about me?" William asked. "I'm practically one of the family."

"My dad thinks you're weird."

"Yep. Practically one of the family," he repeated.

Rolan merely shook his head before taking off.

"So Princess, where do you live?" William asked.

That's right. They've never been to my place before.

I smirked. "In the city."

"Oh, a city girl. I see," William purred.

"I wouldn't say I'm a city girl per say," I muttered.

Giving them directions, we stopped outside the warehouse. Rolan and William looked at it in disbelief.

"You don't live here," William argued.

I climbed out of the car. "Yes, I do."

"But—"

"Mary!" Sera came running out to us.

I smiled brightly and caught her when she jumped into my arms.

"You actually live here?" Rolan asked doubtfully.

"I sure do. Do you want to come in? Maybe we could give you a tour of the place," I said.

William and Rolan followed me in. Once they stepped inside, I heard William gasp. Upon entering, everyone looked at me from around the table where lunch was being served.

"Mary!" Bethany shouted.

"I'm home," I announced.

We had a group hug before we pulled away and they noticed our guests.

"Hey guys," Cassidy greeted. "William, how are you feeling?"

"Better. The burns took longer to heal but they did."

"That's great," Reign smiled.

"Would you like to stay for lunch?" Sera asked. "I could give you a tour afterwards."

"Sounds great."

~X~

I watched in amusement from my position at the dining table as Cassidy and Reign argued again on the couch. Rolan and William had gone home by now since it was almost time for dinner.

"*Criminal Intent* is *not* better then *Special Victims Unit*," Cassidy argued.

"Yes, it is."

"No, it isn't."

"It is so."

"Is not."

"Is to."

"No."

"Yes."

I just watched it go back and forth until they started getting off topic.

"Whatever. Arguing with you will only get us killed...Again!" Reign growled.

"Hey, don't bring that up!" Cassidy yelled. "You were the one that should have just let me pick up the ball."

"But it was my ball! Why should you have gotten to pick it up?"

"It was not *your* ball! It belonged to the foster care woman."

"Yeah who gave it to *me* to play with!"

"Oh, so because she gave you the ball to play with, it was yours and only you could play with it?"

"Yes!"

"That was selfish of you."

"No, it wasn't!"

"Yes, it was!"

"No, it wasn't!"

"Yes, it was!"

I rolled my eyes and I heard Sera sigh as she came down the stairs.

"So Chelsea's Damned Twins are yours too because she doesn't have them on her at the moment?" Cassidy asked, pointing to the two swords on the kitchen bench where Chelsea had been polishing them, leaving only to retrieve her other swords.

"No, but they'd be mine before being yours because I'm better then you at wielding them!"

"No, you're not."

"Yes, I am."

They both eyed the swords.

"Touch my swords and I'll kill you both!" Chelsea called to them from her room upstairs.

Cassidy and Reign looked away awkwardly, not knowing what to do afterwards.

"I have a question," Sera announced. "What is all this 'ball' business anyway? You two always bring it up whenever you have a big argument."

"Don't get me started," Reign groaned.

"I'll happily tell," Cassidy scoffed.

Reign rolled her eyes. "No, I'll do it."

"No. You said to not get you started so I'm telling the story."

"Cassidy!"

"Reign!"

"Someone just tell the damn story!" Bethany snapped.

"Fine."

"Well, it all happened like this..."

"Alright, go have fun!" Kim called.

All the children of the orphanage ran out the back to play. The orphanage had a big backyard for them to play. It was dangerous though because there was a large hole in the wooden fence that lead to the semi-busy road leading into town. All the children knew not to go out there though, so it wasn't too bad.

"Here, Reign," Kim said, handing the purple ball to her.

"It was blue," Cassidy interrupted.

"Was not."

"It was too!"

"Whatever."

"Here, Reign," Kim said, handing the blue *ball to her. "Maybe you can play with Cassidy."*

"Not likely," Reign whispered.

She ran out to the backyard and just played with the ball. She saw Cassidy playing in the sand pit and smirked evilly. She dropped the ball and took aim. She backed away a few steps before running and kicking it. With surprising accuracy, it hit the right side of Cassidy's face. Reign dropped to the ground in a laughing fit as Cassidy gingerly touched her cheek. Tears welled in her eyes but she stood and moved to the ball.

With a reddened cheek and tearing eyes, she kicked the ball as hard as she could. It smacked Reign in the middle of her face, making her nose bleed. Reign let out a whimper as she held her nose. Cassidy ran to the ball that had rebounded off Reign's face and over the wooden fence. Luckily, it was Tuesday, so the road wasn't too busy. Reign, wanting revenge, ran to the ball and both girls reached it at the same time.

"Don't touch it, it's mine," Reign snapped, hitting Cassidy's hand away.

"You shouldn't have kicked it at my face then," Cassidy hissed.

They glared at each other hatefully. When one would attempt to pick it up, the other would hit their hand away. Eventually, Reign pushed Cassidy and they ended up on the ground, slapping and pulling each other's hair.

Out of nowhere, a truck came around the corner, honking its horn for them to get out of the way. It was going too fast to stop in time or for them to move out of the way. They screamed but it did nothing as they were hit and killed instantly.

"And that's the story behind the purple ball," Reign concluded.

"I'm telling you, it was blue," Cassidy argued.

"No, it wasn't."

"Yes, it was."

"Was not."

"Was too!"

"Dinner's ready!" Tori announced over the ruckus.

"Thank god!"

15

JARROD AND ADAM

"**Y**OU'RE KIDDING!" I GASPED.

Jarrod just smirked at me and shook his head.

"I'm serious. He dies by his brother's hand at the end of the fifth season. My condolences," he stated.

I looked at him, confused. "What?"

"Well," he drawled. "I know you had a crush on him."

I blushed. "Shut up. Oh and thanks for the spoiler."

Jarrod Emrys. He was new here a couple of weeks ago but I had never gotten the chance to talk to him until last week. Already, we argue and joke like old friends. He has curly brown hair that is *unbelievably* soft, dark skin –a little darker then my own- and oddly enough, light blue eyes.

I've seen Jarrod get angry once. McFaggot was harassing him when Jarrod's eyes turned gold and slit like a snake. He was breathing deeply and steam seemed to come with every breath. McFaggot practically shit himself and ran.

Funnily enough, that's how we became friends.

"Hey, I saw you make McFaggot shit himself."

"What of it?" He hissed.

I held my hands up in defence. "Whoa, chill out. I just wanted to welcome you to the school and if you ever need someone to hang with, you're welcome to join my friends and I."

He nodded and I held my hand out.

"I'm Mary."

"Jarrod."

He shook my hand but there was a shock that shot up my arm. My eyes widened in surprise and I pulled my hand away from him.

"What the hell was that?" I asked, glaring at him.

He was staring at our hands in surprise before looking up at me.

He scratched the back of his head. "Heh, my bad. I'm a dragon. It happens sometimes."

We liked many of the same things. He's extremely quiet and reserved though, different from me.

He's not as strong in his human body as he is in his dragon form. Not much is known about dragons, only that they serve Draconis, namely the royal family. The dragons you see on TV are pretty much exactly what they look like. Well, so Jarrod tells me. He's shown me his wings. They're maroon in colour, giving away the colour of his scales.

I'm not quite sure why he's here, probably to keep an eye on things I guess. Dragons don't really have any business here at Clandestine Academia and he's not here every day. Just twice a week I'd say.

"You wanted to know," Jarrod stated, bringing my thoughts back to the present.

"Not that much!"

He laughed at me as the bell rang for the end of English Literature. Yay, lunch.

~X~

"Bullshit," Tori stated.

I growled. "Damn it, Tori!" I hissed as I took back the two cards I placed down.

We were playing Bullshit with a pack of cards that Sera brought to school. Why she brought them, I have no idea but this was quite entertaining.

"Two Fours," Chelsea stated.

Currently, Tori was winning. Then it went William, Chelsea, myself and finally, Aura. We decided that it would be safer if the others didn't play since we have such fast reflexes and could hurt one of them. I don't think they minded since they were enjoying the show.

"Bullshit!" Aura called.

Chelsea smirked as she flipped the last two cards she placed on the pile to face upwards. They revealed two Fours.

"Ah, *this* is bullshit!" Aura growled.

"That's why it's *called* Bullshit," Tori laughed.

"You're worse than Mary," Chelsea teased.

"Shut up, you!"

Whispers of the other students caught my attention and I turned to see a handsome teen standing with Camilla in the courtyard. He had auburn coloured hair and blue eyes of ice.

"He's cute," one of the girls whispered.

"Another new student? And this close to the end of the year?"

This piped my interest as I stared at the newbie. He was looking around the courtyard, ignoring whatever Camilla was saying to take in his surroundings and the other students. When his eyes landed on me, he smiled at me and I felt my heart pounding in my chest. Sure, he's not as good looking as Alistair but he was still handsome. He looked away, only for a moment, to mention something to Camilla before she nodded and he looked back to me. My eyes widened when I realised he was actually walking towards us.

"Mary?" Tori asked.

I think it was my turn but who would even think of playing Bullshit when he was walking their way? It wasn't long until he was right behind Chelsea.

"Hi there," he greeted.

Chelsea spun around, swiping her left arm around behind her, also whipping out a dagger in fright.

While we were all waiting for her to mare his perfect-looking skin, none of us were expecting him to actually block the reflex. The moment Chelsea moved, he had his right hand just above her elbow and his left hand holding her wrist, stopping it just in time to avoid having a dagger in his chest.

Sera gasped. "How did you—"

Not only had he successfully blocked Chelsea's attack, he countered it. All he had to do was add pressure to his right hand and he'd snap the elbow at its joint. Chelsea struggled in his grip.

This was no ordinary vampire.

"Let her go," Tori hissed.

The vampire smiled sheepishly as he let her go and stepped back.

"I'm sorry. I shouldn't have snuck up on you like that," he apologised.

Chelsea huffed. "You give yourself too much credit. You didn't sneak up on me. I knew you were coming, I just don't like people behind me."

He continued to smile as he scratched the back of his head. "Yeah, still. Sorry about that."

"It's okay," I answered.

"Anyway, my name's Adam Rade. I'm new here and I was wondering maybe a beautiful young lady like yourself would give me a tour of the place," he said, smiling at me.

"Uh..."

"She'd love to!" Cassidy cut in.

"Well then, shall we get going? There's only so long before lunch ends," Adam stated as he offered me his hand.

Aura giggled as she took the cards from my hands. I took Adam's hand as he helped me up and away from the bench.

"We'll try not to be too long."

~X~

"So where are you from?" I asked.

His smile faltered and was soon replaced by a look of sadness. "I'd rather not say."

He looked like a man who had lived many lifetimes and just wanted it all to end.

"That's fine," I spoke softly. "But if you ever need someone to talk to, I'm always here," I offered.

He smiled thankfully.

"I think you'll like it here. I do. Well, after I got over some of the biased teachers and homicidal students, I started to enjoy myself."

He laughed. "Sounds like you had it rough."

I rolled my eyes. "You have no idea but are you really so surprised? I'm a dhampir. It's the norm for me actually."

He frowned. "So what if you're half human?"

I paused before turning to him. "You don't care?" I asked.

He shook his head. "Why should I? You're a gorgeous girl and from what I can tell, with a personality to match. It doesn't matter if you're half human. It just makes you...unique."

I could only stare at him in awe. I think I felt my heart swell and my eyes tear up. I don't think anyone has ever told me that other than my dad. Not even my friends. Sure, they don't care that I'm a dhampir but they've never called me unique or special.

I was at a loss of words. "I...thank you," was all I managed in the end.

He smiled at me. "You're welcome."

-X-

When the day ended, all I could think about was Adam. He was so kind and gentle and so much like my dad that I couldn't help but connect with him. It was only his first day and I was already starting to crush on him.

Adam is charming, caring and romantic. It's not like me but I dig the romance, something not many know about me. How could they when I enjoy blood-covered clothing and murder? Since my parents' death, I've been obsessed with sending evil vampires to hell. It's funny that I've never really given much thought to my life and how I perceive it.

There isn't a lot the others know about me. They know the shadow of who I am and a brief outline of what made me who I am today. However, they don't know the little things like the fact that I love romance. I want to kiss a guy in the rain. I want to be showered with roses of all colours. I want to fall asleep in the arms of a man holding me possessively. I want to see fireworks when we kiss. But most of all, I want to feel loved.

I've been denied love since I was forced into the life of an orphan. I've surrounded myself with friends to fill the void in my heart left by the passing of my parents. Finally, I meet a guy who may hold just the slightest bit of genuine interest in me and not with the intention to use me. I don't want him to see me as just another one of his mates. That's all I ever end up being; A friend. I'm practically one of the guys. Now that I think about it, I envy my friends.

I jumped when my phone started ringing. I cleared my throat before answering the incisive ringing.

"Hello?"

"It's—....are you okay?" Brenton asked over the receiver.

"Chipper. What's up?"

"There's been another body. It's fresher than the others. Can you be here in twenty minutes?"

"I'll be there in ten."

16

LETTING GO

FOR ONCE, I WOKE UP early. I guess I was so excited to see Adam again that sleep could wait. I ran into the bathroom and showered before getting dressed. I stared in the mirror at my plain reflection and frowned. Maybe I should stop by a cosmetic's shop and by myself some make-up.

I went downstairs and saw Cassidy and Sera cooking breakfast with Chelsea, Tori, Reign and Bethany hanging out on the stools, watching and chatting away about what ever peaked their interest.

"Good morning," I announced.

They turned around. Bethany's mouth dropped open as Cassidy dropped the eggs.

"What?"

"What the *hell* are you doing up?" Tori asked.

"It's...six in the morning," Sera stated.

"Oh my god, the apocalypse is coming," Bethany gasped, eyes wide. "We're all going to die!"

She started shrieking and I rolled my eyes as the others laughed.

"Shut up. It's not that big of a deal, is it?" I asked.

The girls' stopped and just stared at me with a raised eyebrow, including Sera.

I sat down, grumbling. "Bitches."

"So what has you up this early?" Chelsea asked.

Adam flashed through my mind and I blushed, unable to keep the smile from my lips.

"Does this have anything to do with that new guy?" Tori asked.

My silence told them all.

"Naw," the girls cooed.

"Be careful, Mary," Chelsea warned. "I don't want you getting hurt again."

101

My eyes softened when I looked at them all. "Thank you so much for being there for me," I said and I meant it. "I don't know where I'd be without all of you."

Just then, Aimee came down. She stopped on the stairs when she spotted me and raised an eyebrow.

"Should I be worried?" She asked.

I rolled my eyes.

"Screw you all."

-X-

We entered the school grounds and I tried to fight back the urge to search for Adam. Luckily, I was saved the effort when Adam found us.

"Hey," Adam greeted, crooked grin plastered to his lips.

I smiled back. "Hey."

"Well, Mary, are you going to introduce us properly or what?" Chelsea asked, raising an eyebrow.

"Oh, yeah. Adam, these are my best friends; Chelsea, Tori, Sera, Bethany, Cassidy and Reign. You saw them yesterday but I never got a chance to introduce you to them."

Adam nodded his head with a polite smile directed towards them.

"It's a pleasure to meet you all. Mary wouldn't stop talking about you all yesterday," he teased.

I punched him in the shoulder. The girls smiled at us.

"Whatever. Just don't hurt her or I'll hunt you down, got it?" Chelsea threatened.

I looked at Adam who stared her in the eyes.

"I'd be a moron to hurt her," Adam stated, smiling down at me.

"Good. I approve," Tori stated.

All but Chelsea nodded.

She scoffed. "I don't but I'm not going to tell you who to date. If you're happy, I'm happy. If he breaks your heart, I'll break his neck."

Adam didn't seem fazed in the least. Why would he? He stopped Chelsea as easily as stopping a pet. So I guess her threats meant nothing to him. I frowned anyway. I don't want Chelsea to hold any bad feelings towards him. I don't think Adam would hurt me.

The bell rang to stop any other threats and we headed to our classes.

~X~

A few weeks later passed and Adam and I had gotten even closer. He was like another one of my best friends, only my feelings went deeper. I wanted to be more and I think he may want that too.

I arrived at school again with the girls when Adam came to greet us as he usually does.

"Mary, can we talk?" He asked.

I looked at him in concern.

"Is everything okay?" I asked.

"Yeah, I just need to talk to you," he murmured.

"Yeah, of course."

He grabbed my hand and pulled me into an empty classroom.

"What—" I was cut off by a pair of lips.

My eyes widened. It took me a while to register that Adam was kissing me before I closed my eyes and kissed back. While my heart told me that this was right, my soul screamed that it was wrong. It made my stomach queasy and a flash of disgust swept through my body before I buried it.

'*Screw you, Soul. I shouldn't even have you,*' I scowled before Adam pulled away.

"Mary, these past few weeks have been the best weeks of my life. Just thinking about spending time with you makes me happy and eager to come to school, despite some of the horrible vampires that attend Clandestine Academy."

"Adam," I breathed.

"I know it hasn't been a long time but when I'm away, I can't think of anything else but you. You have become my reason for getting up every morning. Please, be mine," he murmured against my lips.

Love exploded inside my heart at the emotions and sincerity in his voice. He held me so possessively that I was becoming weak at the knees. He said the words I always wanted to hear from Alistair. I continued to stare into Adam's eyes for a little while longer. Despite the uneasy feeling in my stomach, I leaned forward and I kissed his lips gently.

"Yes."

He crushed me against him, burying his head in my neck. I wrapped my arms back around him and closed my eyes, smiling. Even though I still loved Alistair, I loved Adam, who was better for me. He loved me for who I was while Alistair just saw me as a piece of meat. It would have never have worked between Alistair and myself and I guess that's why I felt now was the time I had to let Alistair go, once and for all.

-X-

The bell rung and we headed to our form class. We walked to the door and I felt anxious. Since the classroom he pulled me into was in the opposite direction from our form class, we'd be late, meaning everyone would be inside and see us together. I kept staring at the door. Alistair was behind this door. Sure, I've let him go but that doesn't mean I want to go flaunting my new relationship with Adam around, unlike a certain undead whore.

"Are you just going to stare at the door all day?" Adam asked.

I looked up at him to see amusement dancing in his eyes. I released his hand but he held onto mine. He gave it a squeeze and didn't let go. Alright, I guess hiding our relationship was out of the question. He took the initiative and opened the door for me.

Upon entering, the chatter hushed to quiet murmurs as almost all of them stared at the two of us. Adam strode forward, proud to call himself my boyfriend while I followed along, like a child holding onto their mothers hand in a crowded area. Someone wolf-whistled and I looked to see it was William.

"Ooh lala," he sang, wiggling his eyebrows at me.

I burned red with embarrassment and dragged Adam along with me towards William.

"When did this happen?" William asked.

"Just then," I murmured.

"Who asked who?" William asked, turning his gaze to Adam.

"I asked," Adam answered.

"You better treat her right, sweetheart. She means a lot to many people here. Many *powerful* people. If anything should happen to our little princess, it's your balls on the line, understand?"

William's voice was polite and friendly, as was his smile. Creepy.

"I get it."

"Good. That doesn't mean I'm just going to let you get into her pants though."

I choked on air, spluttering. "I—what? William!"

William laughed as he lent over the desk and kissed my forehead. "Did you expect me to say anything less?" He asked.

I thought for a moment. "No. I guess not."

Just then, Adam's phone went off. He pulled it out and looked at the caller I.D.

He turned to me. "Sorry, Mary. I've got to take this. I'll skip form class today," he said.

"Oh. Okay then," I murmured before he raised my head and kissed me.

I went red. The entire class was watching us. Could this be any more embarrassing? Still, I felt fuzzy inside, knowing that he had no problem showing the world that we were together. Slowly, he pulled away.

"I'll see you in second period, okay?"

I only nodded before he was out the door and gone by the time our teacher entered.

-X-

"You seem different tonight," Brenton said, standing next to the body of our latest victim.

The victims were still werewolves, only they have grown in size. That means that the killer is getting either cocky about his ability or he really is getting stronger with every kill. It's a horrible thing to admit, even to myself, but I'm glad the killer is passed the stage of killing small, young children. Even so, too many children were murdered by this psychopath for even god to forgive. This makes seventeen bodies in total.

"No, I don't."

Brenton gave me a blank stare with an eyebrow slightly raised.

"Stop looking at me like that."

"Who is he?"

I gaped at him. "Who told you?"

"You did."

"Damn you."

"No, damn *you*. You're the bloodsucker, not me."

"You're such a dick, *Brent*."

"You too, *pet*."

I growled at him.

"Seriously though. Who is he?"

I glared before sighing. "His name is Adam Rade."

"Oh, yeah? What's he?"

"A vampire."

"Where does he live?"

"I don't know."

"What's he like?"

"Good."

"Who asked who?"

"He asked me."

"Can he fight?"

"Yes?"

"Would I stand a chance against him?"

"No."

"You wound me, *pet*."

"I don't care, *Brent*."

"Does he treat you right?"

"Yes."

"Good for you two," Brenton concluded, smiling at me. "But—"

"There's always a 'but'," I sighed.

"If he hurts you, his ass is mine."

"My, Brenny. I had no idea you were into guys."

"Fuck off!" He spat, disgusted by the notion. "You know what I meant."

"Yeah, I did. But, what's wrong with being gay?" I asked, crossing my arms.

"Nothing. Just that I, personally, would not like to be fucked as such."

"Have you tried it?"

"No!"

"Then don't knock it until you try it."

There was silence between us.

"…have you?" He asked.

I looked at him, confused. "Have I what?"

"You know," he drawled.

"No!"

"Then stop being a hypocrite!"

We both looked at the corpse. I studied it closely, though still disgusted by how mangled the body was. Since the first body was found, no one has recovered any of the missing hearts.

"We're getting closer to catching this bastard," Brenton stated.

But how close is 'close'? How many more people will die, before we catch this bastard?

17

GIRL'S BEST FRIEND

I WATCHED JYE, LEO, KALUM AND Blade as they trained. Aimee stood beside me, assessing them.

"They've gotten better," I stated.

"Well, they had better. I trained them *myself*," she scoffed at me.

"Arrogant much?" I asked.

"Arrogance is overestimating oneself. I don't overestimate. I *know* how powerful I am because I fought tooth and nail to be where I am today," she admitted.

I knew what she meant. Neither one of us sat by idly when we lost everything or had nothing to begin with. We fought with everything we had to survive and continued with life that we gained the right to be confident in our abilities without being called arrogant.

Others outside our group may call us arrogant or cocky because they know nothing and *mean* nothing to either of us. All we knew was that when life knocked us down, we'd get right back up again through blood, sweat and tears.

When she turned to me, the look in her eyes told me she was thinking the same thing I was. She smirked at me and I smiled back.

"Fuck you, Jye."

Our attention turned back to Leo, who was on his ass with Jye standing over him. Jye chuckled as he helped him up.

"Don't be a sore loser," Jye smirked.

Leo tackled him and the two wrestled playfully. We looked to Kalum and Blade and saw the two finish with their jaws at each other's necks. Unlike Jye and Leo, who chose to fight in their human form, Kalum and Blade fought as wolves. They finished with a tie.

"Better," Aimee called to them.

They all finished and stood with Blade and Kalum changing back. I blushed and turned away at the sight of their naked bodies. Aimee tossed them their spare pair of pants.

"You did well tonight," Aimee praised. "We'll call it a night."

The guys cheered before jumping on one another. Aimee rolled her eyes as I laughed at their antics. Then Leo had to get a stupid idea.

"Doggy-pile on Mary!"

"Wha—? Fuck off!" I yelled, turning to run before I fell face-first into the ground.

I turned to see Aimee had taken the initiative to tackle me from behind and lay atop me with the smuggest grin I had ever seen.

"Traitor!"

Before I could say another word, the guys followed.

"Get off me!" I growled. "Do you know how *heavy* you all are? Jesus Christ, you boys need to shower too!"

"She's right," Aimee gagged. "You guys reek."

"Go clean up!"

The boys grumbled before getting off us.

"Oi, race you to the lake," Leo challenged.

"You're on," the other three said in unison before they all took off into the bush.

"Idiots," Aimee snorted, shaking her head. "What are your plans for tonight?" She asked, turning to me.

"Absolutely nothing."

"What's new?" She joked.

"Shut up, you."

"You need more clothes. You have no taste whatsoever so I'm not going to let you go shopping for your own clothes from now on. We'll go shopping tomorrow."

"I don't want to," I whined.

"Don't whine at me. Who said you can't look good when you go hunting?"

"Can't you just go shopping for me?" I asked.

She raised an eyebrow as she put her hands on her hips. Uh-oh.

"Just kidding," I said, laughing nervously with my hands up. "Shopping is good. We'll get dressed and go. It's Late Night tonight."

Aimee smirked at me before turning away.

"The shops in Capalaba are good. Carindale is always overly crowded and I don't like it here in the city. Too many seedy people."

I smiled at that.

"I'll meet you at Central in an hour. Shower and dress nicely. I mean it, Mary. If you show up in an outfit I don't like, I'll strip them off you where you stand."

She would, too.

I gulped. "Understood."

She disappeared into the night and I groaned.

~X~

I stood in the car park of Capalaba Central. I looked at my appearance in the mirror. I wore a pair of black jeans and a black, long sleeved shirt to hide my left arm. For once, my rings glittered nicely in the car park, despite the poor lighting. My shoes were black converses with hot pink laces.

I sensed Aimee inside the shops so I moved forward. I don't know why Aimee thought I'd never been here before. Attending Clandestine Academia here in Capalaba, you get to know the local areas. There are two large shopping centres here. There is Capalaba Central and Capalaba Park. Most of the teenagers here in Capalaba, and even neighbouring suburbs like Alexandra Hills and Cleveland, come here and that's saying something since Alex Hills and Capalaba are like Gryffindor and Slitherin.

Anyway, Capalaba Central is the social hangout around here. They usually meet around the back near the water fountain. If you go out the back, you come to the fountain with stairs around it that head towards the Library. I've been there a few times with Cassidy. It also happens to be that these shops also have a cinema. It's the closest one around here, unless you want to drive fifteen minutes west to the Victoria Point Cinema. I'll admit though, they have better seats.

I found Aimee at KFC ordering food.

"Do you want to get something to eat first?" She asked.

I eyed Hungry Jacks. "Yeah, I'll be back."

After ordering and receiving my meal, I sat down with Aimee on the comfy red leather seats.

"I'll admit that I like it here," Aimee said, breaking the silence. "It's not a big suburb but it's not a small one either. It's…just right."

I nodded. "I know what you mean. It's peaceful and full of humans, ignorant of the supernatural. It's refreshing."

Aimee quickly finished her dinner before tidying up her mess for the cleaners before she grabbed my arm and dragged me away from the table.

"Oh, come on! I didn't even get to finish my burger!" I protested.

"Shop now, eat again later."

She dragged me to Supara. I yanked my hand out of her grip.

"No."

Aimee glared. "Why not?"

"Aimee, you know just as well as I do that this place is for sluts," I spat, staring into the store. "Any store but this one. I have my standards. Besides," I sneered, looking at the girls inside. "I'm sure they don't sell clothes my size."

Aimee sighed. "Fine. How about Alice Girl?" She asked.

I nodded and so we headed there. They had some nice stuff but I didn't get to look since Aimee just pushed me in the dressing room and threw clothes over the door. I rolled my eyes but changed. She made me show her every article of clothing she gave me so I chose to do it properly. When I opened the door, I walked like a model on a runway and stopped to pose. Aimee snorted.

"Good!"

After Alice Girl, we went to Ace. They have some really nice stuff there. By the time we were done, we were carrying bagful's. We headed out to my car and loaded it in.

"Want to stop at MacDonald's?" She asked.

I shook my head. "Nah, but I am keen for a Slurpee," I suggested.

"7Eleven it is."

The trip back home was good with the music up loud and the two of us singing to the words. This was just what I needed and for some reason, I think she needed it more than I did. When we stopped at the lights, I just stared at her. She looked at me and turned the music down.

"What?"

"What's going on?" I asked her.

Something flashed in her eyes before I could recognise it. She turned away from me.

"Nothing," she said, sipping on her Slurpee.

"No, it's something. What's wrong?" I asked. "You didn't take me shopping just to get me new clothes. You needed to get away. What from?"

"Don't worry about it. I'm handling it just fine. I just wanted a break, that's all."

I sighed. "I know I can't force you to tell me anything but we both know you'll tell me eventually. That's why you're my best friend. No matter what, I'm here."

"I know," she murmured.

I turned the music back up and continued through the city towards home. Once I parked my car, we grabbed the clothes and headed inside. When I walked into the main room, I froze.

Everyone sat at the table, only Sera had her head buried in her arms and her shaking told me she was sobbing. I dropped my bag of clothes and was beside her in a nanosecond.

"What happened?" I asked.

Sera didn't move, only kept crying.

"Sera?" I asked gently.

Slowly, she raised her head to me and my eyes widened. Her eyes were red from her crying but what flooded my body with fury, was the bruising around her eye and a cut on her lip. Someone had punched Sera and given her a black eye and split lip.

"Who did this to you?" I asked.

Bethany scooted over from her seat next to Sera and I took her place. I laid my hand on her back.

"Tell me what happened, Sera," I pleaded.

"I went home today because I missed my forest," she sniffed. "When I got home, Byron said his usual mean things. He called my mother a whore and I hit him. He retaliated by kicking me in the stomach and punching me in the face."

"What else?" I asked.

She bit her lip. "She's coming to Clandestine Academia."

"Who is?"

"Roseanna. My sister."

I growled. "Why? Why is she starting at Clandestine Academia?"

"My dad says it won't be long before my sister takes my place as heiress and wants her to be prepared."

I cursed. "Remind me, again, how you could be replaced."

"If I die, become incompetent for leading the Tima family, if I give up my title willingly, or if all the ancient families agree to replace me."

"How is that last one going?" I asked.

"The Queen still sees no reason to replace me."

"I like this queen a lot more," I said and Sera cracked a smile. "Don't worry about it, Sera. If Roseanna is coming to our school, fine. She doesn't scare me and she sure as hell doesn't scare the others. If you like, we could take her out for you," I offered.

Sera looked at me and I could see how tired she was.

"I just want it all to stop," she whispered as more tears welled. "Maybe if I just give Roseanna the title-"

"No!" I yelled, jumping to my feet. "Sera, you can't let them bully you into giving up what is rightfully yours," I stressed.

"Mary's right," Cassidy stated. "If you do, then they'll be right in thinking you were too weak and not only will you disappoint yourself and your mom, but the Queen too. She seems to have faith in you."

Sera looked down at the table.

"Sera," I murmured. "I know it's hard and that you just want to give up. Giving up would be *so* much easier than to deal with all this shit, but I promise you, in the end, it'll all be worth it."

"You will be able to help your family in ways that Byron couldn't. You have a heart of gold and that's what is necessary to lead your family," Reign stated.

"Unlike Byron, you *care* about what happens to your family, so please, no matter what happens, promise me you will *not* give up," I pleaded, holding out my pinkie.

Sera stared at me with her big blue eyes and I watched as thoughts processed in her head. Then I saw her decision and her eyes lit up in determination. She grabbed my pinkie with her own.

Her voice held no doubt in her reply.

"I promise."

Chelsea smirked. "Let's see what this Roseanna brings us."

18

True Story

WE LOOKED AROUND THE COURTYARD when we got to school.

"Hey, babe," Adam greeted as he approached us.

I immediately broke into a smile. He caught me in a hug before he leant down and kissed me. I felt all giddy inside.

"I have a present for you," he stated, pulling out a small velvet box.

When he opened it, I gasped. Inside was a silver ring with a dark blue jewel in the centre, sparkling up at me.

"Adam," I breathed.

He removed it from the box and grabbed my left hand. He went to remove my glove before I pulled my hand away.

"Not that hand," I blurted.

He looked at me, hurt shining in his eyes.

"What's wrong?" He asked.

The look on his face didn't disappear and I felt guilt bubbling inside my chest.

"N-Nothing," I stuttered weakly. "Just not my left hand. It has enough rings on it."

"Oh. Well, okay then. I'll just put this on your right hand."

He took my right hand and slipped the ring on my ring finger. He smiled down at me and I couldn't shake off the feeling that maybe our relationship was a mistake. Gazing over his shoulder, I spotted Alistair with Angela. The two were standing by the bubblers. Angela had her hands on his chest and Alistair's arms were around her waist.

"What's wrong, Mary?" Adam asked.

I looked at him and shook my head.

Here, standing before me, was a man who wanted me. A man who always showed me respect and would have me just the way I am. We always kissed, unlike Alistair who only made out with me.

I smiled at Adam. "Nothing," I sniffed. "I'm just so happy."

He wiped my tears away. "I love you."

More tears fell as he brought me closer, holding me to him. I wrapped my arms around his waist. I don't know why but no matter how many times I tell myself I love him, I just can't speak the words out loud.

-X-

Ancient History with Wrathie was still shit for a second period. After the first lesson about Senina and Audrea, Wrathie went back to the boring stuff. Though today, he decided to keep on the subject. This is our second lesson on the sisters. I sat between Tiny and William.

I jumped in my seat when someone poked me in the ribs.

"Hey," I hissed quietly, turning to William.

He laughed at me. "You seemed pretty into the story. Why the sudden interest?" He asked.

I sighed and leaned into him. He threw one arm around my shoulder. We did it all the time that it was only natural to do it without thinking.

"I like to hear him speak Senina's name," I stated quietly.

He gave me a knowing look. "You miss your Vala?"

I nodded. "Yeah."

I looked up at him.

"Do you think it's safe to start using my real name?" I asked. "I mean, it has been a while."

William went into deep thought for a few minutes. "No. Your father hid you for a reason. His enemies could still be out there," he answered.

I sighed sadly. "Damn."

His arm became firm as he brought me in closer. "If it makes you feel any better, I'll call you Senina when it's just us two."

I smiled at him. "Would you?" I asked.

He nodded. "Only if you call me Felix."

I held my hand out to him. He took it and we shook hands.

"Deal."

"Hazel, stop talking!" Wrathie yelled.

"Sorry."

"What was the name of Senina's two grandchildren?" He asked.

I think this was supposed to be a trick question since he hadn't gotten that far into the story. All we had learnt so far was what made the two vampires and that Audrea was cast out after killing their parents.

"Tomas and Ema."

Many eyes turned to me in shock. I returned their stare.

"What?"

"Hazel, see me after class."

"Goddamn it."

-X-

I stood before Mr Wrath's desk. He sat in his office chair and just stared at me, contemplating something. I stared back with a raised eyebrow.

"Why am I here?" I asked, breaking the silence.

"How do you know about the story of Senina and Audrea?" He asked, not missing a beat.

"You can't answer my question with another question!" I huffed.

He just stared at me. He wasn't going to say anything else so I could either just walk out of here and let him make my life a living hell for the rest of my time here, or I put aside my pride and answer his damn question.

"My dad used to tell it to me when I was a little girl."

"And how did your dad know?" Konan asked.

"Fucked if I know. Why does it matter?" I asked warily.

"Only certain people know all the details to the story. Those are people from either Draconis or Vipera."

"Yeah, well, I already guessed my dad was from one of them. All half-breeds have a True Blood parent."

"What was his name? Perhaps I knew him."

"I'm not going to tell you what my dad's name was."

"Why not?"

"Because he said bad people were after us when I was younger. Mom never called him by his real name, only Love, Dear or Sweetheart. I only called him Dad and I'm assuming I'm still in hiding so I keep my Vala and my dad's Vala to myself."

"Who do you think I'd tell?" He asked.

'Anyone that wants to kill me,' I sneered inwardly.

115

'Make him swear by our goddess, Senina, not to tell a soul and he can be trusted.'

"Swear by Senina's name that you won't tell anyone," I spoke.

Konan's eyes widened slightly before quickly going back to his usual blank face.

"I swear by my goddess, Senina, that I will not speak a word of whatever is said in this room."

'Good.'

I looked at Konan and stared at him, hard.

"His name was Dragomir. Dragomir V. Amare. You can't mention it to anyone, understood?"

Konan's eyes widened. "Dragomir?"

I nodded. "Yeah. Did you know him?" I asked.

He nodded slowly. "Yes. Your Dad was a powerful vampire."

Then his look turned bitter. For some reason, I didn't want to know what he was thinking.

"What kingdom was he from?" I asked.

Konan stared at me.

"Draconis."

I let out a sigh of relief. "Thank god. I've never liked the sound of Vipera."

Konan chuckled.

"What family are you from?" I asked.

He raised an eyebrow. "What makes you think I'm from one of the ancient families?" He asked.

I shot him a look. Really? He really thought I wouldn't know?

"I don't know. Maybe because you just said -not even five minutes ago- that only people under Draconis or Vipera know all the details of the story. You obviously know it and I know most of the teachers here belong to one of the two kingdoms."

He looked at me with surprise, probably because he never thought I could process that amount of information in my half-bred brain. Well then, good. I shocked him.

"Leal."

"So you're like an uncle or something to William?" I asked.

"I'm his father."

My jaw hit the floor and I dropped the books I was holding.

Oh my god. No way was my sweet, sweet, William the son of the bitter, aggressive Konan Wrath. Then I realised that I didn't know what William's last name was.

Oh my god.

William Wrath.

Wrath William.

William.

Wrath.

I refocused on Konan to see the amusement in his eyes. I wonder if he'd still think it was funny if I told him that his son was bisexual. I opened my mouth then closed it again.

Better not.

Then again, he probably already knows since it's no secret about William's sexual exploits. Maybe that's why Konan is such a dick. Hell, maybe Konan is that way too.

I gagged.

I did not need that mental image in my head. Feeling slightly nauseated, I bent down and started picking up my books. Once I recollected them, I smiled weakly before walking out. I began singing in my head in order to forget the mental image I had before I made it to Vampire Studies. I knocked on the door and waited for Richard to answer. When he did, he looked down at me with concern.

"Are you alright, Mary? You look a little pale."

I nodded weakly. "Y-Yeah."

When I entered, I sat with Aura and the lesson began. I paid attention, not because it was interesting, but because it helped me to forget the most disturbing image I'd ever pictured. By the end of the lesson, my head was clear and I no longer felt queasy.

When it came to lunch, I chatted with William.

"I can't believe you never told me," I growled.

He looked at me in confusion. "Told you what?"

"Who your dad was or what your last name is."

He grimaced. "He told you."

"Obviously!"

"Well, to be fair, I did tell you my last name."

"Leal doesn't count!"

"Says who? Are you really angry about me not telling you my last name?"

"No."

"Sure you aren't."

"Shut up!"

"Okay, so I didn't tell you that Mr Wrath was really my dad," he sighed. "I'm sorry. Do you forgive me?"

He gave me the puppy dog pout and I sighed. "How can I not when you're giving me those eyes?"

He broke out into a massive smile. "Love you, Princess."

I rolled my eyes before an earlier question returned to the top of my head.

"Hey, does your dad know you're bisexual?"

He sighed. "Yeah."

"And he's okay with it? Seriously? How the hell did you manage that?"

William shrugged. "I'm not sure myself. Although, I do believe he may have had an idea when I was a child. He caught me several times dressing in my moms' clothing."

I couldn't help the laugh that escaped my lips.

"Enough about me. What about that gorgeous rock on your finger?"

I blushed as I looked at my hand that rested on the desk, the dark blue jewel sparkling in the light. William took my hand and fingered the jewel, sighing.

"Adam may seem like a strange guy but he sure has taste when it comes to jewellery," William praised after inspecting the ring.

I drew my hand back and rested it on top of my other hand on the table. It didn't stay there long before Adam came over to us. He took my hand and kissed the ring.

"Hey, beautiful," he greeted, smiling down at me.

"Hey."

"The ring looks good on you."

I blushed. "Thanks."

He sat down next to me and we all had lunch together.

"Do you have any plans for tonight?" Adam asked.

I turned to him. "No. Why?" I asked.

"Did you want to come to the movies with me tonight?" He asked.

"Sure."

As we were conversing, I noticed Sera's stiff posture. Turning to her, I found her staring at a woman walking towards us. I looked at the girl and noticed she had the same, soft looking chestnut brown hair as Sera, though instead of the kind blue eyes that shimmered with love, there was hard, devious green.

"Seraphina!" Roseanna called happily.

She went to wrap her arms around Sera when Sera raised her hand, stopping her.

"Roseanna, while I wish I could say I am happy to see you, I cannot lie."

"Big sister, it hurts me to hear you say that," Roseanna whimpered, covering her heart with her hand.

Bethany snorted. Roseanna took a second to look at us all carefully.

"These are your friends?" Roseanna asked.

Sera tensed. "Yes," she breathed.

"Wow. Not another fairy in sight," Roseanna commented before her eyes rested on me.

Pure, unaltered disgust shown in her eyes and I knew if she weren't Sera's sister, that was enough provocation for me to kill her where she stood. How could someone related to sweet Seraphina be so hateful and different?

"And you even have a dhampir friend!" She exclaimed. "I'm sure Dad will be interested to hear about her."

Sera bit her lip and for a moment, I saw her eyes flash dangerously.

"I'm sure he would. I'm also sure you can't wait to get home and tell him all about my life here at Clandestine Academia."

"Of course. Dad always takes an interest in your life—"

"That's it," Tori announced.

"I've had enough of your bullshit acting," Chelsea clarified.

"What—"

"We know you're really a bitch in disguise, you two-faced whore," Bethany snapped.

Roseanna's innocent façade gave way to the hideous person she really was.

"Good. It makes me sick just trying to be friendly with you all."

Then she turned to me.

"Especially you, *hybrid*."

I rolled my eyes. "I am no stranger to disgust and hate. But the feeling *is* mutual."

"Just wait until Dad hears about this," Roseanna sneered.

"Go ahead. It's not like he can even think of stopping us from seeing her," I stated.

"Maybe. But he sure can stop her from seeing you."

"Go ahead and see what happens. I will personally hunt you all down and bust her out of the trees you all hide in," I hissed.

Roseanna glared before she stormed off. Sera let out a breath.

"I can't understand how you two could even be remotely related," Tori stated.

"Right!?" I exclaimed. "The two are exact opposites."

"Things won't be pleasant when I go home," Sera sighed.

"Don't worry about it, Daisy," Bethany laughed, using our absurd nickname for her.

"I meant what I said before. If you call to us for help, we will chop down every tree in the forest to find you."

Tears welled in Sera's eyes.

"I love you guys so much," she whispered.

"Naw, group hug!" Bethany yelled.

Sera choked on a laugh as she cried.

19

DOUBLE DATE

I'VE BEEN EDGY LATELY. I hadn't gotten a call from Brenton in a while, neither telling me about any more bodies or lack thereof. The tension was killing me. I think the others noticed it too. It wasn't helping that Adam was almost suffocating me by how attentive he had been of my needs lately. It was like I could never find some time to myself. Roseanna seemed pretty hell bent on making our lives a living hell as well.

Sera had come to them the next day, telling us about how her Dad tried to forbidden her from seeing us and that Sera had finally - for the first time in the fairy's life- went against her Dad's wishes and pretty much told him to go fuck himself.

Okay, so she didn't exactly tell him that, but you get it.

It was a huge deal for us and that was a week ago. Already, Roseanna had taken some of the friends Sera made amongst the other fairies, though the others followed Sera faithfully. Sera had made it abundantly clear to Byron that she was not backing down and that when she was ready, she would not hesitate to claim her right to the throne and take over.

Man, her face was lit up like a Christmas tree when she told us about her stand off against her only two enemies in her life. Her facial expression had been so animated and her voice was so full of triumph that you couldn't help but smile and get excited alongside her. At least now Byron knew that Sera was not someone he could just walk over without meeting resistance. She always had it in her; she just needed that little extra push.

If push comes to shove, she knows that we're there to push back if need be and that we'd never let her fall or stagger back. The gentleness that came with her insecurities had seemingly vanished and she no longer walked around the school with her head bowed, but held high, finally having found her place amongst the supernatural kind. She had grown from a shy teen to a hardened soon-to-be leader in the span of two weeks.

I can't explain how proud I am of her right now.

To add to my problems, Aimee had been seen less and less as of late. I can feel, deep in her mind, the concern and tension she was feeling, like me. I knew that she would come to me eventually. She always does. If she knew a secret or was troubled, no matter what it is, she'll come to me as I'd go to her, though my secrets aren't very secret since all my friends pretty much know what ever goes on in my life.

But it doesn't end there, no. There have been rumours about Alistair and Angela's engagement. It has been publicised amongst all of us and Angela flaunts around how they plan to have the wedding next year. After seeing how badly Roseanna treats Sera and knowing how harsh Byron is, I no longer hold any hard feelings towards Alistair. Instead, those feelings turned to pity. Alistair may be untouchable to everyone here at Clandestine Academia, but the truth was he must not be very strong if he can't stand against his kin, his father in particular. That's the difference between Sera and Alistair. Sera had finally begun to walk her own path while I doubt Alistair will ever break away from his families expectations.

Sad, really.

So now I have to deal with the ignorance of the werewolf murder's case, Roseanna and Byron, Adam, Aimee and finally, Alistair and Angela.

Fuck. My. Life.

-X-

I shouldered my bag as I exited detention. I finally had enough of McFaggot's shit and decked him one. It also happened to be right in the middle of Mr Wrath's lesson. Wrathie wasn't too happy but he didn't have me suspended as some teachers would. Actually, he just smirked and told me I had detention. I don't know what happened to the real Wrathie but I'm *not* complaining. Strangely enough, Wrathie's been a lot more lenient with me than anyone else, even his own son. It either has something to do with me knowing he's Will's old man, or he does it out of respect for my dad.

Well, he doesn't care too much for his son here so I'm going to go ahead and say it was the last one. He did know my dad after all. Who's to say they weren't friends, though I could never see my dad dealing with an asshole like

Wrathie. Might have been a love-hate relationship like the one I share with Tiny. That stupid giant still hasn't forgiven me for the comment I made about the inferior size of his male reproductive organ. I must have hit the nail on the head for him to still be angry. Must be pretty bad. Poor guy.

Anyway, I'm ashamed to say I'm glad it had been Wrathie's class that I whooped McFaggot's ass.

I headed outside and to where my friends were sitting. I stopped when I saw Alistair talking with Will and Rolan. It seemed important before Will playfully punched Alistair. I saw the slightest upturn of his lips.

How long had it been since Alistair was happy? Or smiled? Or even smirked for that matter?

Ever since he started playing the part as Angela's fiancé, he never had the chance to joke around or just chill. It was always so serious when it came to Angela. She didn't notice or even seem to care, so long as she had Alistair and was on her way to becoming a princess of some kind. Could you get any more selfish?

Spotting Angela over by the other rich True Born, I took a deep breath and walked over to them. Alistair was the first to spot my approach before the other two followed his gaze over to me. They tensed.

"Sorry," William apologised.

"No," I stopped him. "You have nothing to apologise for. I don't mind if you guys chat and hang out. Actually, I wanted to see if you wanted to join us for lunch today," I offered.

Swallowing my pride was never an issue. I'm not afraid to admit when I'm wrong or to move passed things by being the first to apologise. It's good to be the bigger person sometimes. *Sometimes.*

William and Rolan looked at me in surprise before looking to Alistair who hadn't taken his eyes off me for a second. I fought the bubbly feeling in my stomach.

'Goddamn it, Mary! You have a boyfriend waiting at the table you just invited him over to! Get a fucking grip!' I mentally screamed at myself.

Alistair watched me for a few moments more before he nodded his head. I turned and headed back to the table with the three True Born following behind. When we got to our table, *everyone* was surprised I had brought Alistair back to the group. I merely smiled at them, showing them my willingness to forgive him.

I saw my girls were less than willing to do the same. Baby steps at a time. The hate radiating off of Tori, Chelsea and Bethany seared me.

Baby, *baby* steps.

When I got back to them, Adam magnetised to my side. He leant down and kissed me.

"I missed you," he murmured into my ear.

I fought the urge to roll my eyes. "You saw me in period five when I got detention. You've been away from me for no more than half an hour."

He's become extremely clingy. While I love the attention, I needed my space.

"I know but I can't stand to be away from you," he stated.

When he turned to Alistair, only then did I let my eyes roll.

"Hey, I don't believe we've been properly introduced. I'm Adam. I was new," Adam greeted, holding his hand out for Alistair to take.

Alistair stared at him, silently evaluating him. He looked to me before looking back at Adam and taking the offered hand.

"Alistair."

"Does this mean you're the newbie in my place?" Adam asked Alistair.

"No, you're still the noob. Alistair has been a part of this group since before you and the other girls came along," William stated.

Adam sighed. "Aww man. Am I always going to be the noob?" He asked.

I patted him on the back. "Yes."

He turned on me before wrapping his arms around my waist.

"Is that so?" He growled.

There were rare moments where Adam seemed to change from clingy and bright to dark and possessive. The mood swings scared me but I did prefer the darker side. It reminded me of-

'Don't even go there!' I screamed at myself.

Adam nuzzled my neck and I sighed. I fought the urge to close my eyes when I remembered we were in public, with Alistair a few metres away none the less.

"Adam, not here," I sighed, pushing on his chest.

"Who cares if people are around? Let them watch," he whispered, nibbling on my neck.

"Okay, Lover Boy. Give the woman some breathing space," William interjected.

Adam growled quietly before he let go of me.

"Don't forget, Mary. You're *mine*," he hissed, glaring at Alistair as he said it.

Usually I find the whole possessiveness thing kind of hot, but I felt highly disturbed when he said it. I chose not to say anything though.

"Is it just me or did things just get awkward?" William asked.

"Mary!"

We all turned to see Aimee headed towards us.

"You're back."

Aimee smiled. "Yeah. I thought it was about time I stopped skipping out on my job as watch dog."

"It's been forever since I last saw you," Aura stated.

"Like I said, I was wagging. Pun intended."

I laughed and she smirked at me.

"So, when are you going to introduce me to that special wolf of yours?" I asked.

Aimee's smirk turned into a dazed smile as she thought of him. "That's actually what I wanted to talk to you about," she spoke. "I want you to meet him tonight. Maybe you'd like to go on a double date?" She asked, looking at Adam.

I looked up to Adam who gave me that sexy smirk of his. "I'm keen if you are."

"Um," I drawled. "Sure."

"Awesome."

Just then, the bell went.

"Well, I'll see you later," Aimee said before walking off.

"We've got HPE," Tiny declared.

"Then let's make like a foetus and head out!" Tori announced.

-X-

I groaned after HPE. Today was brutal. I don't care what people say about Tim being a softy. There is nothing soft about being beaten black and blue. I'd like to think that I can take Timothy but the truth of the matter is that when he wants to cause you bodily harm, he will.

It wasn't exactly a spar though. It was more like endurance. We each had to last fifteen minutes each, blindfolded and ears blocked with ear muffs. None of us came out untouched. Adam wasn't being overprotective either because he decided to ditch this class. He could have at *least* taken me with him.

"Do you need some help?" Alistair asked.

I looked at him. "Yeah, thanks."

After he helped me stand, we stared at each other.

"Alistair, after everything-"

"I don't want you dating Adam."

"-I hope we can be friends."

It took me a few seconds to register what he said. When I did, I felt as if I had been slapped in the face and I reeled back in shock.

"*What?*" I drew back, away from him.

Alistair just stood there, looking at me without emotion.

"I said, I don't want you dating Adam," he repeated, slower.

"No, I know what you said, asshole! I just can't believe the nerve you have to say that to me!"

"He's only using you. He doesn't *love* you."

I was speechless. I didn't know what to say to that. Rolan and William stood a few metres away from us, giving us space.

"Wow," I breathed out. "I don't even know what to say to that."

"Why can't you see that he's only using you?"

"Probably for the same reason I couldn't see that *you* were using me!" I screamed.

Some people turned to stare at us but I couldn't find it within myself to care.

"Mary, you're being immature. This isn't about us, it's about-"

He was cut off when my hand made contact with his face in an open palmed slap. Many turned to watch us but they were the last thing on my mind.

"Mary," I heard my friends coming to me.

"You son of a bitch," I hissed, barely managing to keep from snarling at him. "Immature? You're calling *me* immature!?"

Oh, god. I was going to blow. I felt Senina herself lashing out from within me and it must have been noticeable too because I saw William flinch away from me as teachers approached us cautiously, looking ready to take me out if I decided to go off the deep end.

"How dare you!?" I hissed icily.

The whole room seemed to drop in temperature but the heat of our rage made some of those around us sweat with fear and anxiety.

"You dare to call me immature when it was you who chose to use me to get back at your Dad?"

I saw Alistair clench his hands and grit his teeth. Hit a nerve, did I? Good.

"You have no right to even imply your dislike of me dating Adam. He was there when I needed him and he cares for me like no other male -my father not included- ever has. You'll do well to remember that next time."

With that, I stormed out of class.

-X-

"Mary, get your ass out of bed!" Aimee's voice drifted from outside my door.

I rolled onto my back and stared up at the ceiling. After leaving the school, I'd headed home to be alone.

I rubbed my eyes before throwing myself off the bed. I walked to the door and opened it, coming face to face with a gussied-up Aimee. She wore a green Boston Celtics jersey and white mini-shorts. Her hair was straightened and she had dyed it red but it didn't come out as well as it should have so it's copper in colour.

"You've got to be shitting me. You're not even ready yet? Bitch, please," she hissed and shoved her way into my room.

I didn't have a say in any of the clothing she threw at me.

She pointed towards the bathroom. "Shower. Now."

I rolled my eyes but stopped when she growled. I locked myself in the bathroom and jumped in the shower. I was out a few minutes later and dressed in the clothes she threw at me. I stared at my reflection. I wore a forest green shirt that tied up at the front and black jeans. I opened one of the cabinets. I couldn't help but smile at all the arm length gloves. Digging through them, I found a candy apple green glove.

I shrugged. Why not?

"Done yet?" Aimee called through the door.

"Yeah," I groaned.

I still hadn't done my hair though. It was wet and I didn't want to really straighten it. Aimee walked in and she stared at my hair and I knew she was going through hundreds of ways to style it. Then she jumped me with a brush.

Half an hour later, I was driving us to the bowling alley in Capalaba.

"So Chase and Adam are already there?" I asked.

"Chase is. I don't know about Adam," Aimee stated.

127

I nodded and picked up the speed. It didn't take long to get there. Once the car was parked, we headed inside. The sound of arcade games, people socialising and bowling balls knocking over pins hit us like a smack to the face.

Because we took so long, Adam and Chase came to us.

"Hey, babe," Adam greeted.

"Hey," I answered, giving him a peck on the lips.

"Mary, Adam, this is Chase," Aimee introduced. "Chase, this is my best friend, and her boyfriend, Adam."

Chase had shaggy brown hair and light blue eyes that stood out almost as much as Aimee's. He wore plain, comfortable clothes such as beige cargo pants and black hooded jumper. Very inconspicuous. Brownie points for him.

Adam shook his hand. "Nice to meet you."

Chase nodded. "Yeah, you too."

He was nervous. I wonder why. When he looked at me, he seemed wary, almost tense.

I let out a laugh. "Aimee, what did you tell him about me?" I cackled.

"Only that your protective of me as I am of you."

I rolled my eyes but shook Chase's hand. "Trust me; it's not me you should worry about. If you hurt her, she will eat you alive *herself.*"

Chase cracked a smile then. Ice = Broken.

"Shall we get our bowling shoes on and show these humans how it's done?" Adam asked.

"I'm keen," I stated.

"Let's do it. You two verse me and Mary," Aimee stated.

"No, let's have a battle of species," I argued.

"We all know wolves are better than vampires," Chase teased.

"Oh, is that right?" I asked, crossing my arms. "Adam, let's show them how kick-ass vampires are."

"Sure thing, babe."

~X~

"I don't fucking believe it," I muttered.

We all stared at the scoreboard.

"How is that even possible?" Aimee asked.

She could only shake her head in disbelief.

"We tied," I breathed. "Six. Fucking. Times. How does that even *happen*!?"

"It's totally rigged," Aimee concluded.

After we tied on our first game, the competitive streak inside both Aimee and I kicked in and we did everything we could to win and break the tie. But it never happened. We just kept tying. I resisted the urge to chuck the bowling ball at the screen and turned around.

"How about we play some arcade games?" Chase offered.

"Good idea," Adam agreed.

Both males had to pull us to the games.

"Verse you in basketball?" I asked.

"Bitch, you're on."

To say the night was uneventful would be a lie but now, I'm back in my comfy bed and reading my favourite book series of all time, *Cat and Bones*. I can't believe how alike we are. She's a dhampir, like me. But there are many things that separate us. I've never hated vampires. I've always know that I was a vampire. My parents loved each other. I don't have a super badass boyfriend that was a gigolo some time ago and then the one thing I take pride in most. I love what I am.

Unlike Catherine Crawfield, I've never been ashamed or disgusted about being half vampire. I've never doubted my existence and I don't hate other vampires simply for existing. She's also older. And Bones? Don't get me started. He sounds so sexy with his British vocabulary and confidence. It's just a fabulous book.

'I wonder who would win,' Aimee's voice bounced around in my head. *'Rogue or Red Reaper?'*

I shrugged. "She beats me in looks and sex appeal."

'We would win, hands down,' Senina whispered inside my head. **'Even without my power, you have the advantage of being trained at the age of five. You also have such potent vampire blood in your veins that it makes you stronger than most vampires.'**

That made me feel better.

'Congratulations, Mary. You're stronger than a fictional character from a book,' Aimee sneered.

'A super, special, awesome book,' I shot back.

Wow. That is sad.

20

THE ANNIVERSARY

SEPTEMBER THE FIFTH; BOTH MY favourite and least favourite day. On the fifth is my birthday. It's also the anniversary of my parents' death.

Headed towards Logan Lee, I stopped by a cemetery. I hopped out of the car after grabbing the flowers in the passenger seat and moved towards my parents graves.

The cemetery was a quiet, peaceful place with a breath taking garden to the left. I stood before their tombstone, the one they share. I knew their bodies were buried beneath me. Amelia told me way back then that there was nothing left of them to bury. Their bodies and...limbs had been taken. It was a miracle Amelia was able to secure their jewellery.

"Hey, Mom. Hey, Dad," I whispered. "I'm back. Not much has changed in a year, only the increase of bad Ascuns killed and making more friends."

I smiled weakly, staring into space.

"I now go to Clandestine Academia," I continued. "I've made many more friends there. William, Rolan, Aura, Mikai, Tiny, Ali-" I stopped, almost appalled by keeping him in my friends list. "I have a boyfriend, too. His name is Adam. He's sweet and he told me he loved me. But I don't think I feel the same. I mean, sometimes I can't stand being around him. I get nauseous. Then again, it's probably nothing. I mean, I was in love with Alistair and maybe I still am, no matter how much I hate to admit it."

My phone started going off and I picked it up, my mood dropping exponentially.

"What?" I snapped.

"What's up your - oh. Shit, I forgot it was today," came Chelsea's voice. "Sorry."

"Don't worry about it. What's up?" I asked.

"Something's up with Aimee. Since you're the closest to her, I thought you'd want to know."

I stood from my kneeling position. "Is she at home?"

"Yeah. She just came in and went straight to her room. She didn't acknowledge any of us on her way. It's like she was in a daze."

I nodded to myself. "I'm on my way."

I closed the phone and looked back at the flowers.

"Sorry but I have to go. My friend needs me."

-X-

When I entered the warehouse, everyone -minus Aimee- was in the lounge watching horror movies. They all pointed upstairs simultaneously that had I not felt trickles of Aimee's feelings on the way over, I'd have laughed. On my way home, bits and pieces of Aimee's emotions slipped through her mental wall, which says enough as it is. Something has caused her to become unstable and I needed to find out what.

I ran upstairs and walked to Aimee's room. I knocked then entered. Screw waiting for permission to enter when I know it won't come. I found Aimee lying on her bed, staring out the window. I said nothing as I joined her on the bed and just laid there, catching the scent of salt. She had been crying. I don't know how long we were lying there before Aimee's sniffle broke the silence.

"He's gone."

I rolled onto my side and stared at her back.

"He just left me."

My mind worked to figure out who she was talking about. It didn't take long for me to realise she was talking about Chase.

"The packs becoming unstable and I guess he just didn't want to deal with the pack anymore, but why didn't he take me with him?"

Finally, Aimee turned to face me. Her eyes were red and puffy, contrasting with her bright blue eyes. I grabbed her scarred hand with mine and just held it. She teared up again and I brought her closer so she was crying into my neck. Her mental walls faltered for a bit and more of her wild emotions smacked straight into me. I bit back a gasp and helped take on those feelings. I took in her anger and sadness and let silence settle in her mind. I don't know how long I was lying there but when I looked down, I found Aimee had fallen asleep. Slipping out quietly, I walked back down to the girls whose movie had finished.

131

"How long was I up there?" I asked, confused.

"About two hours," Chelsea informed me.

That surprised me.

"Is she alright?" Tori asked.

I considered the emotions I'd felt from her. "I don't know. She's a wreck at the moment. All I know right now is that something's going on with her pack and that Chase had left."

Cassidy and Reign tensed, both having the same though.

"What?" I asked.

"How sure are you that he left and wasn't taken by that werewolf serial killer?" Cassidy asked.

My eyes widened and I slammed up mental walls to keep it from Aimee.

"No," I murmured.

"I know it's a terrible thing to think of but you need to consider the possibility that maybe Chase had been taken as well."

"But this week's werewolf has already been killed."

"You know that's not really something to go by," Cassidy said sadly.

"But who knows? Maybe he did just leave," Sera offered mercifully but it was too late.

They're right, he's probably dead. He wouldn't leave Aimee without telling her first. He had to have been taken. To be sacrificed.

"Maybe he's not dead yet but they plan on sacrificing him next week," Bethany murmured.

Oh god, she's right. Whipping out my mobile, I dialled in Brenton's number.

"Yeah?"

"We've got a problem."

-X-

We worked overtime, trying to find any clues but came up with nothing. I was currently going over some more case files while the other files were with Adam in the other Ancient History of Vampires class.

Adam was helping me with the cases. I had told him what happened and he offered to help me in any way. It's been five days since the last sacrifice. Any day now, we'll find out if Chase was taken as a sacrifice.

It's Friday and fifth period with Wrathie and he was onto rather gruesome topics which was a nice change to the usual boring lessons he gives. He was talking about rituals. I was safe to go over my files since Tori and Chels sat on either side of me.

"Some rituals are performed to increase a vampires power. Some vampires bond with a werewolf even," he said, giving me a subtle smirk. "But this way is probably the hardest and less gruesome of the lot."

"Why's that?" Amity Vale, a classmate of mine asked.

"As you know, vampires and wolves don't get along well. To some of our kind, they are nothing but dogs. To them, we are bloodsucking murderers."

"Aren't we though?" Royce Mason joked with his friends who all chuckled and patted him on the back.

Konan rolled his eyes. "The point is that the only way to bond with a werewolf is to share blood and soul and have the utmost trust in their partner during the exchange."

"Who would want to bond with a dog?" Royce asked.

"Open-minded people, asshole," Tori stated.

Royce glared at her but didn't dare answer back lest he wanted his book to be shoved so far down his throat, he'd be shitting origami for weeks. Guess he wasn't as dumb as I'd hoped.

Bugger.

"As I was *saying*," Konan hissed, glaring at Royce and Tori. "The most barbaric would be a vampire drinking from an Ascuns's heart. How much power the vampire gets depends on the Ascuns."

I froze and so did my friends.

"Konan," I asked, forgoing the nickname. "Can you tell us what this ritual entails? How is it performed?"

Konan, having heard me call him by his proper name, knew I was serious in my question. Unfortunately, the bell went and everyone began packing up.

"Mary, stay behind."

I sighed in relief and I'd never been so happy to stay back with Wrathie. Once everyone had cleared out, Wrathie handed me the giant book he had on display, Dark Blood Rituals.

"Why do you want to know about the Schimbul?" He asked.

I handed him my files. He flicked through them before frowning angrily.

"So we have a Vipera vampire running around," he murmured to himself.

"What do you mean?" I asked, suddenly urgent. "Vipera is involved?"

He had the answers and I wanted them.

"The Schimbul is a dark ritual passed down in the Vipera vampire line only. There's no way it could be anyone else. They'd take it to the grave if they could."

"Then how do you know about it?" I asked.

"We have our ways."

"No, really," I said, voice deadpan. "Tell me."

"We may or may not have a vampire within our menagerie that may or may not have psychic abilities to possibly divulge such dangerous information from the minds of dangerous Vipera vampires."

I stared at him for a couple of minutes before I cleared my throat.

"Could you be any more irritating?"

I got the hint. Honestly, who wouldn't? But that was just ridiculous.

Konan's face broke out into a wicked grin. Damn that bastard. He was enjoying every moment of my irritation. I pinched the bridge of my nose while my other hand tucked under my arm, supporting it in a way.

"Okay, moving on," I sighed. "So you're telling me someone from Omor or Moarte is responsible?" I asked.

Konan nodded. "Though it doesn't explain the state in which the bodies are found. I can't think of any other Ascuns but a werewolf that could do this."

"But why would a werewolf do this to their own kind?"

"They could be a Nedorit," Konan offered.

Nedorit. Why did that word seem familiar? Oh, that's right. That's the word I've heard some wolves call Aimee. It's a word given to out-casted wolves. I hear many in Aimee's pack address her as such.

"So we have a Nedorit that's helping a Vipera vampire get stronger by handing over one of their own every week?" I wondered. "But why? What does the wolf have to gain?"

"The two could be bonded," Konan stated. "By increasing the vampire's power, it also increases the wolves. The vampire will be far out of sight until the night of the ritual."

"So we look for the wolf?" I asked. "Find the wolf, we find the vampire."

-X-

I paced around with my phone, talking to Brenton about what I'd just found out. When I hung up, I stood there for a moment, relishing in the fact that we were one step closer to solving the case.

"What's up, babe?"

I turned to see Adam standing at the door to the empty classroom I had locked myself up in.

'Don't tell him just yet. Don't get anyone's hopes up,' Senina whispered in my head.

I nodded to Adam. "Nothing," I said, smiling at him.

"You look…relieved."

"I finished Konan's test last period and I'm just happy it's over."

"Then how about you and I go out to celebrate?" He asked.

"Why not? I deserve it," I sighed.

"Good. I'll pick you up at seven."

-X-

I jumped when there was a knock on the door. I wore a strapless, black, formal fishtail dress with a white fur coat over the top to not only shelter me from any cold breezes, but to also hide my left arm that I chose not to cover with a glove. Diamante heels were strapped to my feet in elegant patterns. A pretty flower diamante necklace graced my throat with matching earrings. My hair was up in a fancy up-do and light makeup was applied. That included powder foundation, blush, black eyeliner, pink lip gloss and bronze eye shadow.

Bethany answered the door and came back with Adam who had on a blue polo shirt with the top three buttons undone and black dress pants. He smirked at me and I blushed, looking at the ground.

"Do I look okay?" I asked shyly.

Adam chuckled sensually. "Don't worry, Mary. You look breathtaking, even though we won't be out with most of the public."

"Where *are* we going?"

"It's a surprise."

"I'll see you girls' later, 'kay?"

"Sure thing. You two have fun," Cassidy called.

"Oh, we will," Adam drawled, sending a suggestive smirk my way.

I blushed brightly and turned away, looking to the girls' for help but they just shook their heads at me.

"Go, Mary. Have fun and *live* a little," Bethany stressed, shoving me towards the door.

Adam wrapped an arm around my waist and led me outside to his car. A midnight blue Mercedes Benz convertible. He opened up my car door like a gentleman and I slipped into the passenger side. He jumped into the driver's seat before holding up a thin material.

"What's that?"

"Your blindfold."

"…are you joking?"

"Do I look like I'm joking?"

"With a face like that, it's hard to take you seriously."

Adam's face contorted in hurt.

"I was joking!" I groaned and took the blindfold off him.

"I know. Me too."

I punched him in the arm. "You're such a dick!"

I tied the blindfold around my eyes and he started the car.

"That's why you love me."

And we took off.

"Sure, sure."

"You do love me, don't you?"

"Maybe."

He laughed and turned up the music. Evanescence, the best band in the world. With them, you can never go wrong.

21

SURPRISES

"A RE WE THERE YET?"
    "No."
"Are we there yet?"
"No."
"Are we there yet?"
"Mary, we're still in your damn driveway!"
I couldn't stop laughing. I can be such a brat when I want to be. After laughing for about five minutes, I sighed.
"Are we there yet?"
"Mary, I swear to god—"
"What? What are you going to do?" I taunted. "You're driving."
"Then I'll get you when we get there."
I stopped and let him drive in peace while I sang along to the radio. I lost track of time and before I knew it, the car's engine cut out and the music was stopped.
Silence.
"Adam?"
'I'd try and run if I were you,' Senina spoke.
'What? Why—oh.'
"Mary."
"Hm?"
I jumped out of my seat when I sensed his lunge for me. Thank god I don't care much for seat belts. I landed in the back seat, slightly disoriented before I had to dodge Adam's attack again. I rolled backwards and off the boot but I stumbled on the gravel, forgetting that I wore heels and landed on my ass.
"Oh, Mary," Adam drawled.

I shuffled back but it was useless. When I jumped to my feet and tried to run, he grabbed me around the waist. I let out a squeal of laughter as Adam's fingers began to tickle my sides.

"A-Adam! Let me go!" I laughed.

"No way! I told you, you were going to get it."

"I'm sorry! Just stop! Please, I'm going to pee myself!"

Adam laughed but stopped his tickle ambush. He untied the blindfold and when it slipped away, I found myself standing out the front of a club. Looking at the sign, it told me we were at a small cricket field.

"What are we doing here?" I asked.

"Come," he ignored me and grabbed my hand.

He led me out of the car park and up a hill beside it. The grass hadn't been mowed in what looked to be a couple of years and came up to my waist as we navigated our way through it where it soon ended, creating a small clearing.

"Why did you bring me up here?" I asked.

He stepped aside and I was staring at a romantic candlelit picnic. I gasped in surprise.

"Adam, are you serious?" I asked breathlessly.

I slowly moved to the beautiful layout. There wasn't much light but since we were both vampires, we didn't need much. The grass felt like a curtain, hiding us away from the world. We had this little hideaway all to ourselves. I stood before the romantic dinner.

"Adam, it's beautiful," I whispered in awe.

"Not as beautiful as you," he murmured, holding out a rose to me.

"That's so sweet. Cheesy," I added. "But sweet."

I took the rose before taking my seat on the blanket. Adam took his place across from me.

"So, what's first?" I asked.

He held up two things. Strawberries and chocolate dip.

"That is so cliché," I teased.

"Humour me."

He opened both containers and dipped the strawberry in the syrupy chocolate before holding it to my mouth. I bit down, separating the little leaves from the fruit itself and munching on the strawberry. A little bit of juice dribbled down the side of my mouth but before I could wipe it away, Adam licked it up. I blushed.

Most of the night, I spent blushing until Adam made me stand.

"What now?" I asked.

"Turn around."

I did so and gasped. I could see over the tree tops and in the distance were the lights of the city; specks of gold, white and blue. It held a sense of peace and beauty. Utter tranquillity.

"I know how much you love the city lights," Adam spoke from behind me.

"Thank you for bringing me here, Adam."

"Don't thank me yet. Turn around again."

I turned back and I lost the breath to gasp. Adam was kneeling before me in that tell-tale position.

"Adam..." I managed to get out.

He smiled up at me. "We've only spent a small amount of time together but already I feel as if you have stolen every part of me; heart, mind and soul. When I wake in the morning, it is you I get out of bed for. When I close my eyes, it is you I dream of. When I imagine where I'll be in fifty years' time, it is by your side. Mary Hazel, will you make me the happiest man in the world? Will you marry me?" He asked, pulling out a velvet box and revealing a beautiful silver ring with diamonds and dark blue sapphires.

I couldn't breathe. I couldn't speak but he told me all the words I needed to hear. My mind wanted to process and analyse everything but I couldn't... no, *wouldn't*, let it.

Tears were falling and I must have looked a mess. I clasped my hands together against my chest and nodded slightly.

"What?" Adam asked, hopefully.

"Yes," I spoke shakily, nodding harder. "Yes!"

I jumped on Adam who caught me and spun me around happily. He caught my lips in a passionate, desperate kiss. It may seem like things were going too fast but vampires did things differently. Eternity is a long time and we're quick to find a companion to walk that long and endless path with us.

He pulled away and removed the beautiful ring and held it out to me. I looked at my left hand and at my dads' rings.

'Why not?'

I removed the twin dragon ring that sat on my ring finger and moved it to my pinkie. I held my hand out to Adam who stared at my dads' rings before smiling up at me. He slipped the ring on my engagement finger before kissing it. He grabbed the wine and topped up our glasses before giving me mine.

"To us," he growled huskily.

"To us," I repeated before we tapped our glasses and took a sip.

~X~

We were still laughing half an hour later.

"I have to take a leak, I'll be right back," Adam whispered against my lips before he disappeared down the hill.

I breathed in the fresh air and sighed before a searing pain ran up my spine. I gasped and bent forward, panting.

'What the hell was that!?'

I looked around me, trying to find where my attacker was when I realised that wasn't my pain to feel.

'Who—'

I was hit again by pain but this time, across my face. I let out a cry and touched my cheek but there was no blood.

Suddenly, I wasn't seeing the tall grass around me, but darkened cave walls.

'Where am I?'

Dazedly, I stood and realised I wasn't in control of my body. Hell, it wasn't even my body I was in. A man came into view, looking to be about thirty or so. He was tanned and muscular but short for his age. There was a large claw mark down the right side of his face.

"You bloody whore!" He barked, spitting blood on the floor. "I'll kill you!"

"You can try, you bastard!" I screamed but it wasn't my voice.

It was Aimees'.

She looked to the side and I saw a few bodies -all male- on the ground, torn up and dead and not far from them were the rest of Aimee's small pack. The women were all huddled away, hiding in fear and men standing by them protectively but in a way that couldn't be seen as a challenge to the aggressive wolf.

"You dare attack *me*, your *Alpha*!?"

"You won't be the Alpha for much longer, Carlos! You don't deserve the title!"

We lunged for him but he was faster. He ducked away, practically rubbing it in Aimee's face.

"Who are you to decide who deserves the title of Alpha or not?"

"I'm the only wolf brave enough to face you!" Aimee screamed. "You may have scared the others into submission and they may hate me but no one, and I mean *no one*, gives you the right to touch our women against their will!"

"I can do what I want," he sneered. "That's what it means to be Alpha."

"Then I challenge you," Aimee snapped. "For leadership of the pack!"

"Stand against me? Fine then. Your challenge has been accepted."

I was thrown back, out of her mind then.

"Oh my god," I panted. "I've got to tell Adam and save her."

'There's no time! We need to get to her, now!' Senina screamed at me.

She was right. I jumped up and ran, through the forest in the opposite direction of the cricket field, away from Adam and car park. It was hard navigating through the forest while wearing high heels and constantly feeling stabs of pain in random places.

"Aimee's in trouble! Grab the wolf boys and get them to lead you to her!" I screamed, hoping they heard through all my other raging thoughts.

"What's going on?" Chelsea asked over the violent current that was my thoughts.

"Aimee's fighting her Alpha!"

"God, I'm not going to make it on foot," I sobbed. "There's got to be some way—Jarrod!" I gasped in realisation.

Still running with Haste, I pulled out my phone and dialled in Jarrod's number.

"Hello?"

"Jarrod, I need your help!" I panted.

"What is it? What's wrong?" He asked, alert to my tone.

"My best friend is in trouble and I can't get to her on foot. I need you to fly me to her. Can you do that for me?"

"Yes, of course. Anything."

He hung up but I couldn't stop running. I had to keep going, to get to where Aimee was.

'Don't worry. We'll get to her on time. You made the right decision to call Jarrod. He'll help us get there.'

I nodded but kept going. Running through the Cleveland traffic, I was in Alex Hills and still going.

"Mary!" A voice called from above.

I looked up to see Jarrod there with his lethal maroon coloured wings. I ran into a darkened park before Jarrod swept down and grabbed my hand. Tossing me up, he manoeuvred me onto his back, nestled safely between his wings with my arms around his neck to keep myself from falling. Higher and higher, his powerful wings took us so as not to allow the human population to see us.

"Where to?" He asked.

"That way," I said, pointing to the west where I felt Aimee.

Jarrod nodded and we drifted back for an extra boost before we were speeding in the mentioned direction. I lost track of where exactly we headed as I focused on Aimee.

"Damn it, Aimee," I hissed, worried.

Jarrod flew faster than the speed of sound, dodging bats and late night birds like a pro. A few of his barrel rolls left me dizzy but I had no time to think about my stomach that was steadily becoming upset. Mentally checking my persons, I found I had no weapons on me whatsoever. Goddamn it all.

"Mary, you don't even need weapons," Tori informed me. *"You're half vampire. Screw mans weapons, use your own."*

She had a point. Look out, Carlos, or whoever the fuck you are. You don't mess with my friends and live to tell the tale.

22

MEETING THE PACK

AFTER THE WORST FIVE MINUTES of my life, we landed in a forest. A couple of seconds later, Cassidy and Reign teleported before us in a bright flash of light. I immediately noticed the duffle bag both were holding, sharing the weight.

"Sorry," Reign apologised. "We had to wait until you reached your destination."

"Why?"

"There was no point trying to get here ourselves. An angels' flight speed is nothing compared to that of a dragons," Cassidy explained.

I looked to Jarrod who had the smuggest look on his face. I rolled my eyes. Grabbing my guns out of the duffle bag they brought, I loaded them before slipping a couple of magazines into my bra. It stuck out awkwardly and it would have been better of me to slip it into my coat pocket but since I never planned on wearing it in, it seemed pointless.

It was a pricey jacket and white. It'd be hell to wash out the blood. Not to mention it restricted my movements. I ripped the heels off of my feet. Now *those* I didn't care about.

Once done, I stood barefoot on the grass with nothing but my strapless black dress.

"Do you want me to come in?" Jarrod asked.

"No, I'll be fine. From what I saw, there was only one vicious dog in there," I spat before pain hit my spine.

I hissed and arched my back, trying to ease the inflammation.

"Mary, what's going on?" Cassidy asked, concern weaved into her voice.

"I have to go," I grunted before running inside the small entrance of a rock formation.

Once inside, I followed the tunnel in complete darkness, before I spotted a speck of light. Running to get to it, I was blinded for a second before I could see Beast Aimee's motionless body, lying in a puddle of her own blood with other wolves around her.

"Aimee!" I called upon impulse, accidentally bringing all attention to me. Every wolf turned to me, growling and snarling as if I had taken their bone. Raising my guns, I shook my head. "Move and I'll blow you all to hell."

"Who are you? How did you find us?" One barked out at me.

"I don't want you, I want her," I said, looking at Aimee who was paling with every passing second.

"You can't take her!" A girl screamed at me. "She's our Alpha! You can't take her away from us!"

"*Your* Alpha?" I snapped. "Last I heard, you all treated her like shit! No, she's coming with me. She's my best friend and I'm not about to let her die!"

"*Best friend*!?" A boy snapped. "With *you*!? A *bloodsucker*!?"

"*Half*-bloodsucker," I corrected. "Yes. We're bound. I saw the pain she was in and I saw that *none* of you bothered to help her!" I snapped. "Just give me my best friend!"

They looked at each other.

"She speaks the truth, I smell Aimee all over her," the male wolf behind me spoke up.

The rest reluctantly backed away and I moved to Aimee. I never lowered my guns, in case one of these pups decided to go *Jacob Black* on me and try to rip my throat out.

'*Girls, come in now,*' I gave the order.

Cassidy and Reign teleported in while I heard others coming through the tunnel before all the others came into view. With them as backup, I felt comfortable enough to lower my weapons as Sera, Cassidy and Reign joined me. They immediately went to work but something was wrong.

"What is it?" I asked.

"We can't heal her properly," Reign informed me. "Because she's in her beast form, our magic has no effect on her. We managed to close the worst of her wounds but she still needs medical attention as soon as possible."

"Shit," I cursed.

This brought on a new problem. Because she was stuck in her beast form until she wakes up, we can't take her to a normal hospital.

"What the hell are we going to do then?" I seethed.

"Actually," the wolf that helped me spoke up. "There's a clinic close by that deals with all our injuries. The doctor is aware of Ascuns and has helped us many times. I'm sure he'll help Aimee."

Not one to be picky in such a dire situation, I agreed.

"We need to be careful not to move her too much," I spoke.

"How do we move her then?" Tori asked.

"Cassidy, Sera and I could do it," Reign answered, her plan unveiling in my head.

I nodded. "That seems like the best way," I answered.

The two angels let loose their wings before Cassidy grabbed Aimee's feet while Reign supported Aimee's head and shoulders. Sera sprouted her beautiful fairy wings before standing at Aimee's side.

"Bethany, some wind to push her up."

Bethany nodded and silver bled into her eyes. The wind picked up around us before Aimee's body was lifted into the air slowly with Cassidy and Reign rising with her, their wings flapping elegantly. When she was high enough, Sera slipped underneath and applied pressure to her back to stop her body from arching and disturbing her injuries.

"Now quickly pass through the tunnel. If you go slowly, you may injure yourselves trying to get out of the enclosed space," I said, turning to Cassidy. "And you're badly claustrophobic. Make it quick and smooth."

The girls nodded. Sera picked up her legs while her wings fluttered like a hummingbirds wings. Then, they disappeared out of the tunnel as Bethany let the wind ease away. We all followed them out to see they did exactly as I asked. Cassidy only looked slightly put off but nothing too bad.

"Alright, show us to this clinic," Chelsea ordered, turning to the male wolf that was being the most helpful to us.

He nodded and changed before leading the way. Tori, Chelsea and Bethany jumped onto Blade, Leo and Jye's back while Jarrod's wings burst of his back and he grabbed me around the waist before taking off into the air.

We watched them closely and I could tell Jarrod hated the pace that was set for him to follow.

"Jarrod?"

"Hm?"

"I...thanks," I answered, my eyes never leaving Aimee's bloody body.

I felt tears coming to my eyes as the thought of how close I am to losing her kicked in.

"If you hadn't come to help me, I don't know what would have happened to Aimee."

I looked up at Jarrod who smiled down at me. "Mary, I'll always come when you call."

"But why?"

"You're my best friend," he shrugged. "I've never had a friend before and then you came along."

I laughed as I wiped away my tears. "Hey, it's not like you get off easy. You have to put up with the craziness that follows me everywhere."

"That I do."

"Just...thanks, Jarrod."

"No prob."

Moving a bit, I realised his hold around my waist. "Jarrod, aren't I heavy?" I wondered.

Jarrod raised an eyebrow at me. "Mary, I'm a bloody dragon. I could carry two elephants if I wanted to. Besides, there's nothing wrong with you or your weight."

"Says you who is like as skinny as a twig. How do you do it?"

"I have a fast metabolism," he shrugged.

I sighed. "Of course you do."

After a little while, we saw a small building near the main road. The driveway was long but only dirt. I'm assuming he doesn't get patients from the main road but the bush that surrounded his house because that was the exact route the others were taking.

Once they reached the house, Jarrod took us down as the assisting wolf knocked on the back door.

"Reece, we need to go back," one of the wolves said. "Dean and Alan will stay here to watch over her."

Reece nodded to her before the back door opened. A blonde teenage boy stepped out. He had beady brown eyes that reminded me of one of the stuffed teddy bears I had as a kid.

"Cody?" Jye asked.

Cody looked at Jye with wide eyes. "Jye?"

"Cody, is your dad home?" Reece asked.

The blonde turned to Reece and then to Aimees' motionless form. "Yeah, come in."

"Chelsea and I'll go scout the area and make sure that whoever was responsible isn't planning on coming back," Tori stated.

I nodded. "His name is Carlos and if you do happen to come across him, don't kill him. Bring him back to me."

"I'll go with you girls," Jarrod stated.

They nodded and Jarrod disappeared into the pitch black sky as the girls vanished into the bush around us. We entered the house and Cody led us to an empty room while calling for his dad. Aimee was placed down on her stomach before the three girls moved away from her.

It wasn't long before a tall man that looked a lot like Cody entered. His hair was longer, framing his face, bright cerulean eyes protected behind a pair of reading glasses and he donned the typical doctors' jacket. If he had black hair and dark brown eyes, he'd be my stereotypical scientist/doctor.

"Hello. I'm Dr Banner," he introduced as he moved to Aimees' side.

After checking her over, he straightened from his bent position with a frown on his face.

"I'd like to talk to someone who knows about these wounds. The rest can wait outside."

I looked at Reece, my wolves and friends. "I'll stay," I told them.

The doctor walked to Reece where they talked quietly, about Aimee most likely.

"What do you want us to do?" Reign asked.

"You guys wait for Chelsea and Tori to finish their area clearance before heading home. There's nothing more we can do. I just want to stay with Aimee."

"What about Jarrod? Do you want me to send him home?" Cassidy asked.

"Could you?"

"Of course."

"Thank you for coming and could you tell Jarrod that I owe him?"

"Sure. When will you be home?"

"I don't know yet."

"We have school tomorrow but we won't make you go. That's probably the last thing you want to think about," Reign murmured.

"You're right."

"Alright, well, if you're not back by two o'clock, we'll call you to make sure you're okay."

"Okay."

They hugged me and said their goodbyes to Aimee before walking out. I turned to my wolf boys.

"We're going to wait outside and catch up with Cody," Leo stated.

"Old friends?" I asked.

"Yeah. It's been a couple of years since we saw him," Jye answered.

"Alright. How long will you stay?"

"For as long as you do," Kalum murmured.

"Are you sure?"

"Yeah," Blade ended the conversation before they walked out as well.

"Alright, I have to go," Reece stated, bringing my attention to the remaining two people in the room aside from myself. "We'll leave two wolves here to keep an eye on her."

"Why?" I asked. "Before Carlos, none of you gave a fuck about her. Now, after being mauled by your psychotic Alpha, you do. Why? Why now?"

He looked away in shame. "I know."

"Then?"

"She's technically our Alpha now."

"So that's it?"

"No," he huffed. "After everything we put her through, after all the shit we gave her, she still stood up for us, for the pack. She faced Carlos when no one else had the guts to. She fought for the pack and almost died for it."

I continued to glare at him before turning away. "Fine, but you better hope to god that she makes it through this because if she doesn't, I may take it out on your pack that only *now* realised how dedicated she was."

He said nothing as he turned away but I wasn't finished.

"What happened to Chase?"

He froze before looking at the ground, his back still to me.

"He left to protect Aimee."

I raised an eyebrow as I turned to fully face him. "What are you talking about?" I asked firmly.

"Carlos, he had already started targeting some of the males. Chase opposed him and obviously, Carlos didn't like that. So he threatened the one thing he cared about, more so than the pack."

"Aimee."

Reece nodded. "Yeah. He left so that Carlos would leave Aimee alone."

"Where did he go?" I asked.

"The Northern Territory."

"Will he be back?"

"If someone goes and gets him, yes."

"Will someone go get him?"

"Maybe."

"Get him."

"Maybe."

"It wasn't a question."

Reece turned around, glaring at me.

"Don't tell me—"

"Don't start. Aimee was heartbroken when he left. She thought he left because of her. She needs all the support she can get and if I wasn't needed here by her side, I'd get him myself."

"How come we've never heard of your bond before tonight?"

"Because you already treated her as an outsider. It would have only added fuel to the fire."

"Yeah," he muttered. "I guess you're right."

With that, he left but I knew he would do as I asked and bring Chase back. Aimee needed him as much as she needed me and we both knew it.

I turned to the doctor who was rechecking all of her wounds again. "So, what's up?"

"She has many severe wounds. I'm going to need to stitch some of these and that will help her heal but there is something strange about these wounds."

"Why?"

"Something's preventing her from healing. What made these wounds?"

"Another werewolf."

"But that's impossible. Werewolves don't possess the ability to interrupt the rapid healing components in another werewolf's genes."

"So..."

"Either he poisoned his claws, is diseased, or is a new species of werewolf."

"He didn't look any different."

"That may be so but it could be that underneath that fur is something more deadly."

He left the room before coming back with an electric razor. I watched as he carefully shaved away the bloodied silver fur, revealing the large gash underneath. It looked as bad as it felt, starting just under the nape of her neck and ending at her lower back. I knew it was going to scar and that it'll show up on her human body. I watched as he cleaned it, slight stinging stabbing at my back before he started disinfecting it. I tensed as the pain coursed through my veins.

"Can't you just block your bond between you two?" Dr Banner asked.

"I can," I winced. "But I like to think she can feel me there, in her mind. She holding onto our bond at the moment so if I have to suffer in order for her to live, so be it."

"Interesting little thing, aren't you?"

I chuckled before hissing in pain again.

"Tell me, what's it like being bound to a werewolf?" He asked.

I sat in the chair by the bed and held onto Aimees' paw, letting her know I was there mentally *and* physically as the doctor prepared to stitch up the wound.

"It's just like she's another part of my soul. We share two souls, pretty much."

"There mustn't be many secrets between the two of you."

"We respect each others privacy, as well as the ability to block the other out."

"How did you two meet?"

"I'll answer that if you answer my question first."

"Go ahead."

"How come you're human and Cody's a werewolf?" I asked. "I can sense that he's a full-blooded werewolf and not a half-breed like me."

"It's a long story."

"So is mine. Give me the short version."

"Cody was bit by a werewolf when he was four."

"And he survived?" I asked, shocked. "He wasn't mauled?"

"No. The wolf was actually saving his life. Cody was swimming in a river while we were camping and he swam out a little too far and was taken by the current. We didn't know he was gone because he had wondered out of the tent during the middle of the night," he spoke as he started to stitch up the large gash on her back.

I grit my teeth from the pain but focused on his story to distract myself.

"We woke to his cries for help and followed it down to the river. There was a large waterfall and Julie -my wife- dove in to get him. They both fell down the waterfall, a twenty metre drop and I thought I lost them both. When I got down the bottom, I saw my wife's body on the bank with a large wolf standing over her. Her body was broken and I knew she was dead the moment I saw her but Cody was just hanging on. There was no way he would live, being so far out in the wilderness. After looking at the two, I realised the wolf had pulled them from the water. She pierced Cody's arm with a fang gently, if that's even possible. She nudged him a little with her nose before picking him up and out of Julie's arms by his clothes in her mouth. I thought she was going to take him but instead, she moved away from the spray of the waterfall and curled up around Cody."

"What did you do then?"

"I pulled Julie's body away from the water and moved to the wolf. I was hoping for a miracle as I prayed for my wife that was now with god in heaven and that she'd leave Cody with me. I'll never forget staring up at the full moon and crying. Then the next day, Cody started crying. The wolf looked at me and I swear she nodded. I ignored my instincts telling me to stay away from her and took Cody who was uninjured and alive. He would be with me for many years to come."

"Have you seen the wolf since?" I asked.

"Yes. I see her by the house sometimes, checking on the pup she made and when she does, I send Cody out to spend the night with her."

"You don't mind him being a werewolf?"

"No. I'd rather he be alive and a werewolf then dead and human."

"I wish humanity and the undead were as understanding and accepting as you."

"So how did you and Aimee meet?"

I spent the night with Cameron -Dr Banner- telling the story of how Aimee and I met and also about my wolves who were with his son, even after he finished tending to Aimee's injures but I knew. I knew that with Dr Cameron Banner, I had nothing to worry about. Aimee would go through this and she would live.

23

Past Connections

"MARY, WAKE UP."

Raising my head, I looked into Konan's pitch black eyes.

"Sorry," I muttered, sitting up and tried to focus on him.

He frowned but didn't say anything more. As he continued on with the lesson, I stared at my left ring finger, where my engagement ring should have been. I'd taken it off before I entered the school grounds. With Aimee still in Cameron's intensive care, I didn't feel like stirring up a fuss. When the bell rang, I gathered my books and headed to my next class. While in the hall, I reached into my pocket to pull out the very ring I had been thinking about.

"Mary, wait up!" William called.

I spun around in shock and made to slip my ring back into my pocket but before I could, William stopped me.

"What have you got there?" He asked.

"Nothing."

"You can't lie to me, Princess."

"I'm serious."

"Your right index finger just twitched. It does that when you lie."

"Bullshit."

"Sorry, sweet cheeks, it's the truth. That's why you always lose games that require bluffing."

I huffed and turned away, slipping the ring into my jacket pocket subtly.

"I saw that."

I spun around, frustrated. "William…"

"You know I'm just playing with you."

Before I knew it, he was before me, looking at me with that caring look I assume all older brothers share with their younger siblings.

"I heard about Aimee," he murmured softly, placing a hand on my head.

"Who told you?"

"You know Tori can't help telling me everything."

"Yeah…"

"How are you holding up, sweetie?"

"Not too well," I sighed.

His hand moved to cup my cheek and I leaned into his touch. I was just so tired; tired of everything. Who would have thought my life would become so bloody complicated when all I wanted was to protect my friend?

"Hey," William tipped my head back by my chin so that I was looking into his eyes. "Keep your head up, okay?"

I didn't want to but I nodded anyway. William smiled at me. It was one of those smiles that told you everything would be okay and I found myself hoping he was right. That everything *would* be alright. He slung an arm over my shoulder and led me out to our table.

"How is everything between you and Adam?" He asked. "Did your date go well?" He asked.

Thinking back on it, I smiled and blushed.

"You wouldn't happen to be smiling about this, would you?" William asked as we got to our table.

When I looked at him, I saw him inspecting my engagement ring.

"W-What…" I gasped, reaching into my jackets' pocket to find it missing. "William!"

"He proposed!?" William shouted excitedly.

I flinched from his loud voice and looked around to see everyone in the courtyard looking at us.

"W-William, would you be quiet?"

"What's going on? Who proposed?" Tori asked from the table.

William held out the ring to them. "Adam! Adam proposed! They're engaged now!"

"What?!" My friends shouted, standing from their seats.

"When did this happen?" Aura asked.

"Why didn't you tell us?" Bethany asked.

"I'll take that," a voice spoke softly amongst all the yelling.

Turning, I saw Adam snatch up the ring from William before wrapping an arm around my waist.

"I proposed on our date," he answered for me.

I smiled up at him as he pulled me close to him. He bent down and caught my lips before his right hand raised my left one and slipped the ring on.

"And she said yes," he murmured against my lips.

"Adam…" I sighed, wanting to just wrap myself with him and forget about everything.

Our friends cheered around us and I broke away, slightly embarrassed. The girls hugged me while the boys shook hands with Adam. I looked at the girls that surrounded me, I couldn't stop smiling. I looked over their shoulder and saw Alistair with Angela and for once, I felt nothing.

No pain. No sadness. No anger. No nothing.

And I couldn't be happier.

-X-

"I heard about Aimee."

I sighed and rolled my eyes as I looked up at Konan. He was kind enough to let me read the book on dark blood rituals during the lunch break. William wouldn't shut up about my being engaged.

"Has *everyone* heard about Aimee? As a matter of fact, how the hell did *you* hear about that?"

"I have eyes and ears everywhere, Mary."

I stared at Konan blankly.

After a moment, he sighed. "I heard William say something to Rolan."

I smirked at him as he looked slightly disgruntled.

"Yeah, she was attacked by her Alpha," I spoke, changing the subject back. "Some Alpha…"

"Right?"

An awkward silence settled over us.

"Why is she still in a coma? Shouldn't she have healed by now?" He brought up.

"Yeah, but the doc said that something was preventing her from healing; that maybe Carlos had poisoned his claws or evolved somehow."

Konan merely raised his eyebrow in question but I shrugged him off.

"Don't ask me, I have no idea myself."

The werewolves' next evolution? The thought alone scared me.

Lunch came to an end with the bell. I looked down at the book before getting up to move to my next class.

"Could I borrow this?" I asked.

Konan's face took on a strange expression. Even though he was looking at me, it was like he wasn't seeing me at all and I don't mean deep in thought or *staring into my soul*. He was looking at me with familiarity.

His lips curled into a smirk and I was suddenly hit with the realization that he was quite handsome when he forwent the angry, stuck up, prick attitude.

"Your father was one of my best friends, did I tell you that?" He asked.

Ah...

"That explains the look."

His turned to one of confusion, looking at me questioningly. "What look?"

I smirked and he rolled his eyes.

"As I was saying, your father and I grew up together."

"I don't care much for his past or family," I cut in. "You people cast him out for being his own person."

For once, Konan looked put-off.

"Did Drake tell you that?" Konan asked.

I looked at him funnily. "Drake?"

Konan raised an eyebrow. "Drake is your father's alias; Drake V. Lovering."

"*Lovering*!?"

Konan chuckled. "Yes, I remember when we first picked out names. We teased him about the name but he'd just smile."

"Konan," I murmured, my thoughts drifting off to my father. "What happened between my father and his family?"

Konan sighed and lent further back in his chair, his eyes trained on the ceiling as he recalled memories from what I figured to be so long ago.

"Your dad had only three friends that he cared the world for; myself, Ana and Anthony. He also had a younger brother that he also adored."

"I have an uncle? Dad never said anything..."

Konan nodded. "In a nutshell, your father was betrothed to my sister, Ana, but his brother was in love with her, even though Drake and Ana shared some kind of romantic feelings. We took him out to help him forget about it all and he met your mother, Mel."

Konan began to chuckle.

"Your mother was being attacked in a dark alleyway and your father, wanting to be the Knight-in-Shining-Armour, flew to her rescue, but it wasn't needed. Your mother was a black belt in karate. By the time Drake got there, Mel had already kicked his ass."

I couldn't stop the smile that lifted my lips. I never knew my mother was a black belt but somehow, I'm not surprised. Now that I think about, she was quite physical.

"Since that day, your father became enamoured with her and he chased her for months before she agreed to 'date his undead ass'."

"Wait, when did my mother find out about father being a vampire?"

"The day they met. It's hard to explain glowing red eyes and elongated fangs. He didn't have much control since it was his first time outside of Tavina."

Konan sighed again. "Anyway, your parents started dating, meanwhile Cezar, your grandfather, was arranging for him to wed Ana. But one day, Ana grew curious as to why Drake kept disappearing. Unknown to us, she followed us to meet Mel. The next time I saw Ana, she was exiting Cezar's study and she had Drake's journal that held all of his special memories and important events that happened."

Instantly, I made the connection. "She told on my father."

Konan nodded. "Cezar was furious when he read Drake's journal, about his human lover and called a Vechi Adunare."

I frowned. "An ancient gathering, right?" I recalled.

Konan nodded again. "And before everyone in the court, his father read out his journal entry about Mel and in our society-"

"-what he was doing was practically taboo," I finished and Konan nodded.

"Faced with his so called 'crime', Drake was ordered to never see her again and that the marriage was moved to the next day, but Drake refused. He was in love and nothing, not even his father, could stop him from being happy. His father banished him and he left, but not after saying goodbye to Costin who he encouraged to take his place as Ana's betrothed."

I stood silently as I let the information sink in.

"Did they get married?"

"What was that?" Konan asked, turning his head to look at me.

"Ana and Cosmin. Did they get married?"

Konan nodded. "But when news arrived that Drake had been killed, Ana went to find him."

I froze when I thought back to that time and who exactly had come.

"Ana isn't her Vala, her vampire name, is it?"

It wasn't a question.

"No."

I took a deep breath. "Her name was Amelia, wasn't it?"

Konan's quick head movement to look at me answered my question.

"You saw her?"

I held his gaze but didn't say a word.

"After she went looking for Drake, she vanished and never came back. What happened to her?" Konan asked, suddenly standing.

"She was killed."

"What?"

"It is true, she came to find my fathers' body but she didn't just find him, she found me too."

Konan stared at me with his mouth agape.

"She took me in and trained me. She taught me how to survive and fight. She taught me everything I needed to know now that my parents weren't around to teach me."

"How did she die?"

"We were attacked while out hunting by a vampire called Dorin. We both attacked him but he was stronger and killed her but not before she dealt an almost fatal wound to his stomach. The wound left him weak and he fled, leaving me to live another day."

Konan ran a distressed hand through his hair with a shaky breath.

"I'm sorry," and I meant it.

"I guess I knew she had been dead for a while. I just didn't want to believe it..."

I moved to stand right in front of desk and bowed my head respectfully. "Your sister was the strongest and bravest woman I'd ever had the pleasure of meeting. If it weren't for her, I would have died from starvation beside my parents since I had refused to move. She fed me, clothed me, protected me and trained me and I am forever in her debt and in turn, her family's debt."

Konan reached over his desk and placed a hand on my head, slowly tussling my hair like a teacher would to an accomplished student.

"Your parents... your *father* would be proud, Mary."

24

ON THE EDGE

LATER THAT NIGHT, I SPENT the whole night reading about Schimbul and I
felt like there was something I was missing, a connection I wasn't making.
But for the life of me, I couldn't figure it out and it was driving me crazy.

Multiple werewolf lives were counting on me and I wasn't pulling
through!

Out of frustration, I threw the wine glass I had been sipping from, not
flinching from the crash as it shattered against the door.

"Damn it!" I cursed.

A knock on the assaulted door snapped me out of my insanity.

"What is it?" I called.

"There's someone here to see you, Mary," I heard Sera say timidly through
the door and for a moment I felt a small amount of guilt.

"I'll be down in a minute," I sighed.

"Are you...okay?" Came her reply a moment later.

No.

"Yes."

"Do you want me to stay and help you clean up the glass?"

Yes.

"No."

Help me.

"I'm fine, Sera."

Please, don't go.

"Alright, I'll leave you to it."

Come back!

I shook with the raging emotions inside me and I just felt like pulling my
hair out or breaking more things. With a growl, I punched the wall. I wasn't
surprised to see it give way under my fist, though I didn't extract it from the

hole. I panted, staring at the wall. My eyes flickered agitatedly as my fangs pierced my lip when I bit down slightly.

"D-Damn it," I hissed as angry tears spilt down my cheeks.

Nothing was going right! I felt like everything was slipping between my fingers, like I couldn't keep a grip on anything.

'Aimee, the murders, Adam, Alistair, Angela, Amelia, Father-ugh! Damn it all!'

My frustration kept rising and I couldn't understand why I was getting so angry. I buried my head in my hands when I caught sight of Adam's rings and they were the last things I wanted to see right now.

I tore his rings off my fingers and threw them at my desk. I choked on a sob as I cradled my left hand that held my fathers two rings. The instant the rings hit my desk, immediately I was filled with regret.

It wasn't Adams' fault that I couldn't figure this out. Before I could grab his rings, I heard Tori calling me to hurry up.

I took one last look at the damage my room had taken before rushing down the stairs and my eyes widened when I took note of who was standing in my home.

Chase.

-X-

"Would you like something to drink?" Cassidy asked.

Chase shook his head politely. "No, thank you. I'm good."

Standing before Chase, I watched him.

"Have you gone to see Aimee?" I asked him.

He shook his head. "Not yet. Reece informed me of what's happened and so I came here to give you as much information about Carlos as I can before I go to her since I don't plan to leave her side anytime soon."

Despite everything, I couldn't help but smile at this man so devoted to my best friend.

"She's lucky to have you," I stated.

He smiled. "Not as lucky as I am to have her."

"Now, about Carlos?" I asked.

"Carlos was a rogue wolf before he came to our pack around April. As soon as he found us, he challenged our previous Alpha, Mira," he began. "He won but he was brutal. He dragged out her defeat. Beating her within an inch of her life before practically tearing her apart. But then he attacked her pup so that he wouldn't oppose his rule when he grew up. He was only ten. No one knew what to do. We knew he'd just kill us for the sake of it if we so much as thought about disobeying him."

"So you guys just let him stay Alpha?" Reign scoffed.

"You don't understand. His strength was nothing we had ever seen before. He was stronger then anyone we had ever met. He was faster *and* stronger then us. There was nothing we could do without it costing many lives."

"Why did he send you away?"

"I was the Beta of the pack for Mira. Carlos decided to keep me as Beta but on a short leash and had me doing border patrol until he decided I could stop. I was the second strongest in the pack. At least, that's what I thought," he murmured. "Is it true Aimee stood up to him and even managed to hold him off?" He asked incredulously.

I nodded. "She fought hard for your pack."

"But if she was even close to being on par with him, she's got to be the strongest our pack has to offer. Before I left, I had to watch him forcefully take some of our females. Heck, one of them -Magda- is pregnant with his pup."

"That explains why Aimee was so upset these last couple of months."

He nodded before he stood up and dusted off his pants, a subconscious sign of leaving.

"Thank you for coming," I said.

He nodded and I followed him to the front door after grabbing an apple, anything to keep my hands from fiddling. Opening the door, I found it to be pouring bucket loads.

"Mary?"

My attention went back to Chase who stood in the rain, staring ahead.

"Yes?" My voice was weak and for the first time, I let show how hopeless I felt.

Chase looked over his shoulder at me.

"Don't give up," he murmured.

I suddenly felt like there was something stuck in my throat, finding it hard to swallow or speak.

For several moments I stood there, struggling.

"But-" my voice cracked and I knew I couldn't finish.

Chase turned to face me full on. "Like Carlos, Aimee is different. She healed faster and when she really reached deep, she was a better wolf. These passed few months, Aimee has changed for the better. She has surpassed me in strength, she's more perceptive but most importantly, she 1s opened up to others."

He continued talking, but something he said caught my attention.

Like Carlos, Aimee is different.

The only thing that is different between Aimee and other werewolves was her spiritual bond to me. And suddenly, everything made sense.

"Mary?"

My head shot up to see Chase looking at me with concern. I felt something hit my foot and realised I had dropped the apple.

"You have the same look Aimee gets when she remembers something," he said cautiously.

"Carlos," I murmured.

"What was that?"

"Carlos," I said louder, looking Chase in the eyes, everything becoming to blindingly clear. "Carlos!" I exclaimed. "It's Carlos! Carlos is one of the Werewolf killers!"

Chase became more alert and I dragged him back inside to the others.

"Everyone, front and centre!"

In seconds, I had all of the girls gathered before me with Chase. I began the long explanation.

"It's Carlos that's killing the werewolves!"

They all came to life at that statement.

"What? Are you sure!?" Cassidy interjected.

I nodded. "It makes sense now! The reason why he's so much stronger, the reason why Aimee isn't healing like she should be? Carlos is bonded to a vampire like me and Aimee. His partner is the Vipera vampire, performing the Schimbul!"

"The what?" Chase looked at me, his eyes screaming confusion.

I darted upstairs to grab the large book Konan lent to me. I slammed it down onto the table in my haste, causing Sera and Cassidy to flinch from the sudden loud noise. I wasted no time finding the page about the Schimbul ritual, which wasn't hard considering I had bookmarked it. When I opened to the page, it revealed the atrocity of the ritual and the main sticky notes I left to help me keep up with my investigation. I stepped back and allowed them to read it while I stood there and ran over everything in my mind and tried to help by explaining it my way.

"The Schimbul is a dark ritual, forbidden even. It requires the body of an Ascuns. The one performing the ritual must forcibly remove the Ascuns' heart, while they are conscious. Pain and fear cause our instincts and power to increase from adrenaline. The more pain they are in, the stronger the results of the ritual."

"That explains why most -if not all- of the bodies were mangled," Tori spoke.

I nodded. "Exactly. Now this investigation began early this year around late March, early April and Carlos..." I trailed, directing my gaze to Chase whose eyes widened when he saw the proof before him.

"Arrived around April," he finished for me and I nodded.

"But only the Vipera can perform this ritual," Chelsea stated.

"Which is where I suspect a bond like mine and Aimee's comes into play," I announced.

"That would explain why Aimee is having problems healing," Reign murmured. "With the added power from the ritual, it's bound to give him some kind of advantages."

We all stood there in eerie silence. I myself couldn't believe what a breakthrough we had made. Months of tracking these bastards and we finally have some headway!

"Wait," Chase mumbled but there was something in his voice that froze my insides. "So if you're right, which I'm afraid you very well might be, the man that attacked Aimee is the one responsible for the murder of so many werewolves."

While it did seem like a stupid observation, I immediately caught on to what he was trying to say. I felt dread fill me and my stomach drop.

"Which means he'll come back for her," I whispered shakily.

Suddenly, we were rushing around the house, grabbing our weapons. As we rushed out into the pouring rain, I prayed that we made it in time.

25

THE HUNT

A S WE REACHED THE HIDDEN clinic, I knew straight away something was wrong, if the two bodies of dead guards were any indication. Looking at Chase, I noted the tensing of his body, holding himself back from transforming out of anger. The fact that he hadn't showed me the extent of his control and that he understood that running head first into the clinic wouldn't be smart. At all.

Looking to those behind me I held a finger to my lips, not that they needed me to tell them to be silent. Pointing to Tori and Chels, I gestured to go around back. With a nod, they stealthily disappeared around back. I know I could have talked to them telepathically, but Chase would have had no clue what was going on, so for his benefit, I used gestures.

There were only two doors into the clinic but there were many windows. With a look to Bethany, she nodded and added air pressure on the windows, stopping anyone from escaping that way. If anyone tried, they'd find the glass unbreakable. Seeing the angels and fairy as standby healers, I made a move.

Stalking forward slowly, I entered the clinic where the glass door should have been. Taking care to check rooms I passed, I slowly entered further. The bodies of those meant to guard Aimee littered the floors, broken and bleeding, though none lived. Blood painted the walls, the ground and even splatters of blood had reached the roof. It looked like no one within the clinic had been spared. There was an odd alarm, shrill and unchanging, one long sound.

But it didn't take long before I was able to pick up the sound of erratic breathing hidden by the alarm in one of the rooms.

Gliding around the shattered glass on the floor, I managed a peak.

"Cameron!"

I moved to Cameron who had been trying to patch up Cody, who was a bloody mess on the examination bed. Cameron himself wasn't looking too good either. His left arm was badly scratched and the back of his white coat was dark with blood. The blood caused the coat to stick to him, but I could still make out the four claw marks.

"Mary! Oh, thank god," he wheezed.

I helped him to another bed but forced him to lay down on his stomach.

"You stay here, the girls will tend to Cody," I assured him.

His face seemed to relax a little before tensing again and his face twisted in pain.

"You, on the other hand, are infected," I murmured, spotting the grey tinge his skin was turning around the wound.

Tori and Chels entered behind the others.

"The clinic is all clear," Chelsea declared.

"But Aimee's gone," Tori added gravely.

"Fuck!" I cursed.

Sera came to stand beside me as I peeled away Cameron's ruined coat, revealing a lean but toned back, which surprised me. Cameron hissed quietly in pain, but otherwise made no move to stop me.

"Can you tell us what happened, Doc?" Chase asked.

"Everything was going fine tonight and it was relatively peaceful, apart from the storm passing over us," Cameron began, pausing every now and then as I tried to disinfect the scratches on his back. "It was probably because of the storm that we didn't hear him coming and the rain must have covered up his scent since the other wolves couldn't smell him."

"Carlos, right?"

He nodded weakly. "Yeah. He barrelled in and the slaughter began. We weren't prepared. Cody was beaten down, almost dead but I took a couple of hits for him and dragged ourselves into this room. But I did see him run out with Aimee."

"If we leave now, we might be able to catch them!" Chase cried.

I nodded. "You're right. Tori, Chels, Reign, you three on me. Sera and Cassidy, you two patch Cody and Cameron up as much as you can considering your healing powers won't work because of Carlos's power. Bethany, protect them."

"What about me? I'm coming with you," Chase argued.

I shook my head. "No, you need to stay and help protect them. Plus I need you to keep an eye on Cameron. He's infected and you're the only one that can help him."

"But I-"

"I'll get her back, Chase," I assured him. "I promise."

He looked ready to challenge me on it but thankfully, he backed down.

"Alright, fine."

"Thank you. Once the Banners' are able to be moved, take them back to your pack and be ready, just in case. Inform them of the truth about Carlos."

Chase nodded and I looked to Tori, Chels and Reign before we turned to leave.

"Be careful, whatever you do," Cassidy spoke, clearly worried and I couldn't help but smile at her.

"Same to you guys. Take care."

~X~

"I've got the trail," Tori called over the rain and rumble of the storm above us.

"So tell me again why you don't just track her through the bond?" Chelsea scowled.

"Because she's unconscious. Without her consciousness, our bond is thin, asleep. I can feel her pain and whatnot, but because she herself isn't entirely *there*, I don't know where she is."

"So she isn't waking from pain?" Tori asked. "That's not a good sign."

"It's not too bad. She would have been pumped full of morphine or some kind of painkiller. The pain is small, just a dull throb."

"We should try and catch Carlos before he has a chance to give Aimee to the vampire since they'll be harder to track then," Chelsea informed.

"But we can't go too fast or we'll miss something," Reign shot back.

As we trekked in relative silence and shadow, we followed the trail of low broken tree branches and flattened brush.

Frustrated, I flicked the hair out of my face, huffing.

"Should we call the dogs?" Chels asked.

I frowned. "You should stop calling them that. They could take offense to it."

She shrugged. "Well they *are* canines."

"There's a difference between dogs and wolves, Chelsea," Tori chuckled.

"Not a big difference."

Allowing the banter to ease my nerves, I tried to look further ahead but the rain was coming down too hard, not to mention it was dark.

"To think, the murderer was closer then we ever imagined," Reign spoke up from behind me.

"Kind of terrifying if you think about it. This whole time, their alpha was taking other werewolves and mutilating them."

"Jeez, Tori. Don't sound too enthusiastic."

"I'm just saying!"

"Wait, shush!" I called, spotting a light up ahead.

"What is it?"

As we moved closer, slower this time, I could see it was a rundown, old cabin with the front porch light on. We paused just before the clearing of the front yard, staying hidden behind the cover of the brush and shadows.

"I have a bad feeling about this," Reign spoke weakly.

"We can't stop now."

Slowly, we moved out of the long grass and towards the house. Tori and Chels moved to check either sides of the house while Reign stayed by me. We waited out the front in the light, my guns ready and aiming at the front door.

"Mary," Reign whispered.

She was tense behind me, I could sense that but her voice shook.

"What?"

"Behind me," she almost whimpered.

I felt my heart stop for a moment and my stomach sink as terror seized me.

'No, no, no, don't do that. Think!' I mentally shouted but my rain-drenched body refused to move. *'O-Okay, a plan! All we need is a plan.'*

But there wasn't any time.

Opening the link, I called to her. *"Reign, when I say, dive to my right side. Try getting as far in front of me as you can."*

I didn't wait for her reply as I flexed my fingers around the handles of my guns.

"MOVE!"

Senina's roar through my mind caught me by surprise, spooking me into action. As I spun left to face behind me, I felt Reign's arm brush my shoes, meaning she must have heard Senina too.

I didn't have much time to think about it because once I had a view of what stood behind me, I was glad I was going by instinct.

A large beast stood before me. It stood on muscular legs and had a large, solid looking chest. It towered over me, my head reaching the middle of his chest. His arms were long, as were his claws. His hands reached his mid-thigh and his nails continued to just below his shin. His mouth was open as he panted, huffs of steam coming from him while also revealing his razor like teeth. His black eyes stared deep into mine, as if he wanted to devour my soul through my eyes. He was hunched, looking every bit the wild beast he was.

My head screamed to flee but my instincts had me sending bullets in his direction. The beast swiftly dodged before disappearing into the brush around us, hiding in the shadows we had just come out of.

"Reign, get into the air. It's not safe down here," I ordered.

She didn't need to be told twice because not a second later she was taking to the skies. Knowing she was out of harms way, I spread out my arms, my guns trained on the bush on either side of me while my eyes searched in front. I couldn't rely on my sight since the light coming from behind me left the bush in pitch black darkness and my hearing was filled with the sound of the skies tears touching ground.

Fighting the fear that pushed for my eyes to stay open and alert (no matter the fact that I couldn't see anything outside the light's perimeter), I closed my eyes.

Alright, Mary. Focus,' I told myself, trying to rein in my panic.

As I surrendered to my Third Eye, a breath I hadn't known I'd been holding left my lungs in a deep exhale.

This time, there was no words from Senina, only the action as my body rolled to the left, feeling the air on my right shift as something rush through the spot where I had once been. With no time to think, I flipped backwards, springing off my hands before landing on my feet, followed by a duck and a cartwheel to the right.

The sudden sound of gunfire threw my focus and my eyes instinctively snapped open mid-dodge. The distraction hindered my speed and I felt a pain shoot through my head as I was grabbed by my hair and yanked up, dangling in the air. My left hand naturally dropped the gun it had been holding to grip my hair, trying to relinquish the pain while my other hand pointed the gun at it's chest and fired several rounds. Once my magazine had been emptied, I struggled in its grasp when it's free hand wrapped around my throat.

I gasped for air as the mutant dog squeezed, feeling my windpipe constricting.

"Chelsea! Tori!" I heard Reign scream. "Help her!"

Dots darker then the shadows themselves appeared in my vision as my body began to weaken. My eyes rolled upwards, where I could see Reign keeping herself up with every powerful flap of her wings. Red tinged my sight as Hysteria tried to kick in, but this time, it was too late.

"Run...away..." I wheezed as the energy left my body, my arms and legs falling limp, giving up the fight.

'Is this...the end?'

26

DESPERATION

M Y ARM FELL AWAY AS I fought just to keep consciousness. All I could
do now was gurgle and hiss while my pulse thumped in my ear.
I heard a piercing screech and then -through the black spots and tunnel
vision- saw a flash of silver gleam right before my eyes and I dropped like a
sack of potatoes.

Suddenly every sense snapped back to attention like a rubber band and I
was wheezing, struggling to breathe. My hand shook as I held it to my throat
as I forcibly took gulps of air at the same time as coughing like a 40-year-old
smoker. I'm sure I scratched up my throat with all that excitement.

When I finally had enough sense to look up from the spot of grass my gaze
had focused on while trying to breathe, I saw Tori kneeling over me, worry
in her eyes and the sound of fluttering cloth and the clinks of metal. One
panicked look towards the sound revealed it was the sound of Chelsea moving
around the beast in a deadly dance of claws and swords.

I tried to wave Tori off. "Don't worry about me. Go cover Chelsea's six."

Tori hesitated before she looked towards Chelsea's fight, which she
was slowly starting to lose as the beast's overwhelming strength dominated
Chelsea's grace. Tori looked around quickly before she disappeared. When she
came back, she had three long vines that she expertly wove into a rope. When
Chelsea was slammed against a tree, Tori struck.

She sprung into action, barrelling into the giant wolf's head, knocking him
back. She maneuverer herself so she landed on her back and the wolf above
her. Her knees had been brought up, pushing against his shoulder blades while
she had the ropes wound around her arms and wrapped around his neck. She
extended her balled form, increasing tension on the rope and pressure around
his neck, trying to strangle him.

Not seemingly bothered at all, Carlos reached up and cut the rope and some skin with his claws. He flipped over and with a swipe -as if he were batting away a fly- sent her crashing into the house.

"Tori!" I wheezed.

Big mistake. Carlos turned his attention back to me. Movement behind him caught my attention and I could only stare in surprise as Reign hovered above. My combat-trained eye spotted her intentions immediately. She was keeping purposely out of his sight. She was going to attack him.

And she would be killed.

Carlos towered over my pathetic form, having still not recovered from a partially crushed windpipe.

"Reign, don't-" I forced my damaged cords to yell but it was too late.

Reign swooped down and vanished from my sight. Carlos suddenly howled in pain, his body convulsing and arching. Flickering purple light came from behind him as his bellowing cry continued. From the light and sound, it sounded like he was being electrocuted. After what seemed like minutes but what was probably only a couple of seconds, Carlos fell.

Forwards.

My eyes widened as he fell and I could have sworn if Aimee were here, she'd have yelled 'timber'. Before I could be crushed by his weight, however, Chelsea slammed into his side with a roar, propelling him to the right where he crumpled instead of landing on top of me.

I stared at Chelsea in wonder for a moment as she tried to stand straight but a pain in her gut made her flinch back to a hunched stance.

"Not my most graceful moment," she admitted.

A weak groan came from behind me and I looked back to see Tori staggering towards us, arm broken and leg bleeding.

"What the hell just happened?" She slurred.

I looked forward to see Reign hovering in the air. In her hands was a purple, flickering orb.

"What is that?" I croaked.

My gaze flicked up from the flaming orb to Reign who was white as a bone. She stared in horror at the object in her hands.

"It's his soul," she murmured.

"But why is it purple and not blue?"

A whisper, but it sent a shiver down our spines.

"Because he's still alive."

-X-

We all stood around the table, staring at the soul in the middle. Tori, Chels and I had been patched up, thanks to Cassidy and Sera's healing magic.

"How is this even possible?" Tori asked.

"That's the thing," Cassidy spoke. "It *shouldn't* be possible."

"Well there is a living, *breathing* beast chained up in our basement while his soul is up here," I snapped. "And I want to know why."

After getting over the shock of an angel holding a soul of the living instead of the dead, we managed to drag ourselves and Carlos home where we chained him up, down in our cellar with silver chains.

"What do we do with it?" Sera asked.

Cassidy hesitated a moment before she reached for it. I don't know if any of us were surprised or not that her hand went straight through it, unable to pick it up.

With a look shared between the two angels, Reign extended her hand and scooped up the soul.

"So only Reign can pick it up?" Tori spoke aloud.

"You should go to Celestia," Sera suggested.

"Celestia?" I wondered. "Is that someone who can help them?"

"Celestia is not a person, but a place," Cassidy answered instead. "It is where the angels go for proper training in Tavina; the Celestia Temple."

"Celestia can wait," Reign finally spoke up. "There is no better teacher than experience."

"What are we going to do about Carlos?" Chelsea asked.

"You, Tori and Reign are going to force the information out of him."

"Why don't we just kill him?" Reign frowned. "If he's bonded to the psychopathic vampire, wouldn't it kill him as well?"

"If what Konan says is true about the vampire being Vipera, then he would have had access to all the dark rituals. Who's to say he doesn't know a ritual that can cancel that affect on him? From what I've experienced with Aimee, the process would be inevitable, but slow. He would have time to perform the other ritual to cut ties with Carlos."

"And he would use Aimee," Cassidy finished for me.

"Exactly."

"But through Carlos, we can find his bond mate," Sera stated.

I nodded. Everyone seemed to be on the same page now.

"We will do what needs to be done," Chels assured me before the three of them left.

"You should get some rest," Cassidy spoke, concern ringing in her voice.

I sent her a small smile and a nod before bidding the others goodnight and then heading for my room upstairs. The next few days were going to be hell.

-X-

My eyes snapped open, searching the room frantically.

'Where am I? What happened?'

All I could see was pitch black.

"Mary, can you hear me!?"

I bolted upright in my bed. Those had been Aimee's memories. She was the one in the dark room and she had just woken up.

"Aimee? Aimee, I'm here!"

"I'm losing consciousness again," she whispered into my mind, as if her kidnapper would hear her thoughts.

With his dark magic rituals, it wouldn't be surprising.

"No, stay awake!" I pleaded. *"Aimee, stay with me!"*

"I can't. I'm sorry, Mary."

I wiped furiously at the tears that had began to spill.

"I will find you, Aimee," I swore. *"I promise, I will find you."*

All was silent on her end and I thought she had lost consciousness before she could hear me, but she whispered back, her thoughts affectionate and watery.

"I know..."

Rolling out of bed, I dressed quickly before hastily making my way down into the cellar where cries of pain could be heard. Entering the cell, I found Carlos chained down on a table, spread out as Tori dragged a silver dagger down his chest.

"Still nothing, Hun," she informed me.

"I ain't tellin' you shit!"

I glared at the beast on the table. "How about when we remove those lovely fingers of yours?" I hissed lowly.

"I think I have an idea," a voice called.

Turning to the cell's entrance, Reign stood there holding Carlos' soul.

"W-What is that?" Carlos grunted out through the pain, staring at the purple orb.

"Nothing you need to concern yourself with, mongrel," Tori chimed.

Carlos growled from where he lay before Chelsea cut a finger off.

"Aa, none of that," she said, grinning wickedly.

"What's this plan of yours?"

"From what you've told us," she began. *"The bond you share with Aimee is practically intertwined with Aimee's soul, yes?"*

I nodded my answer.

"As we have found out, Carlos is bonded also. A bond that ties one soul to another must leave a mark."

I took a moment to roll her words around in my head. *"You think you'll be able to find this mark?"*

"I think I already have."

She gestured with her head to leave and I sent a look to the two vampires. Chelsea nodded while Tori smirked.

"Alright, big guy. Let's have some fun, yeah?"

Reign and I headed back upstairs as Carlos let out a pain-filled scream.

27

Fight Against Time

Aside from Chels and Tori, we all stood at the table again as Reign played around with the soul. She kept touching it, moving it every which way.

Finally she let out a shaky breath, clutching the soul to her chest with her free arm extended and fingers curled around something unseen to us, perhaps even to her.

"I've got a hold of the bond," she murmured, most of her concentration on the soul.

"What do you want to do?" Cassidy asked.

"Sera and Bethany will gather the wolves," I ordered. "Cassidy and Tori will grab William and the others. Chels, I want you to go to the Clinic and have Cameron on stand by, if he's recovered from the Change. We don't know how badly injured Aimee is so we need him to be ready in case it's an emergency."

"What about you? You and Reign aren't going to confront the vampire on your own, are you?" Sera asked, eyes shining with worry.

I shook my head. "No, we're going to follow this lead. If it turns out to be right, I'll call for you all. This guy has been collecting too much power to be taken lightly. We will need every ally we have."

They all nodded and I looked at them all, concern filling my eyes.

"Be careful. We're all going to take down this bastard and get Aimee back. Safely," I stressed. "Everyone comes home alive and in one piece."

Even as they nodded, I saw the doubt reflecting in their eyes. This vampire was unlike anything we've ever faced before and god only knows what the dark ritual did to him. Clearing my throat, my back straightened as I double-checked my guns.

"Alright, let's move," I declared. "Happy hunting."

-X-

Reign and I moved quickly while still cautious. Even so, the pace wasn't fast enough for my liking.

"Look, I don't want to mess up, okay?" Reign snapped at me after my latest request to hurry up. "You seem to forget that this is my first time doing *anything* like this."

"But-"

"Let me *breathe*, woman!"

I cursed and looked away as I trailed behind her. I took a look around the streets before she led us through a small valley where large drain pipes released rain water. I felt a tugging at the back of my mind, startling me to a stop.

"Aimee's awake," I told the annoyed angel before me.

When she turned to me, her previous frustration had been replaced with concern.

"Do you want to follow the bond you two share?"

"There's not much I can do. All I'm getting from the bond is pain."

She didn't continue on the topic but she did pick up her speed, much to my relief. Unfortunately, I let my guard down as we rushed through a valley.

A dagger came flying out of no where, aimed at my heart. It never made impact because I was shoved out of the way, followed by a cry of pain. I was up in a second, spotting the dagger buried up to the hilt in Reign's shoulder.

We weren't given any other warning as several vampires appeared in the valley around us. All I could do was draw my guns.

"Shit," Reign cursed under her breath. "I can't do anything one-handed, but if I let go of the soul, I think it's going to return to Carlos."

"You're sure?" I asked, eyeing those around us.

"Yeah," came her reply. "Even now, I can feel it pulling back towards home."

"Can't we just destroy it?"

"It's our only lead."

"Damn it all," I growled. "Take to the sky."

Without another word, Reign's wings burst from her back before she took off, spiralling upwards to safety. Her departure seemed to be the starting gun as they all moved. Releasing control, I gave in to my animal instincts, letting it explode from the fear that boiled away in my stomach.

It was like the receptors in my eyes mutated as my vision changed. The sky turned red while all unimportant objects darkened to black, shadows that didn't interest me. The men that surrounded me shaded to snow white and above me, Reign turned gold thanks to Chelsea's blood.

Now that I had time to explore and experience more of the Hysteria stage, I learnt how to hold onto some semblance of control. After coming to understand the basic, primal urge to survive, I'm now able to activate it at will but only twice with a large interval in between. My body can't take the strain of it for too long. Even controlling it took every ounce of mental strength, to the point of cutting off from the Link. It was only due to Chelsea's blood I take into my body weekly that kept me connected to Reign enough to recognise her as an ally.

The best way for me to describe it is like a mother with her child. When the child is in danger, suddenly the mother has the strength to rip the car seat out if the car breaks down on train tracks or if the child is stuck under a car and the woman finds the power to lift the vehicle up and off them.

The muscles in my body that aren't essential in my survival shut down so that more blood can be pumped to the parts I need most, like my arms and legs. Because battle required most muscles, my body ends up running low on blood so my natural instinct is also to replenish and the only way to do that during combat is to take it from my attackers.

So when I effortlessly tore off someone's arm and held it above me to allow the blood to pour down my dry throat, I didn't let it bother me.

Time had slowed down for me due to my focus being at its peak and I watched them all, even as my thirst was still slowly being quenched thanks to the detached limb.

They didn't seem to realise what they were up against.

-X-

Reign landed behind me but I couldn't tear myself away from the strangers throat I'd latched onto.

"Are you alright?" The angel asked, her voice soft and hesitant.

I held a hand up in her direction for her to stop and stay away, at least until I had some semblance of control again. That control didn't return until five bloodless bodies later.

Gasping for breath, I pulled away from my last victim, my thirst quenched yet exhausted, despite the fresh blood inside me.

"Alright," I puffed. "Let's get moving."

Looking at Reign, I finally realised she'd been injured and was recovering on the ground. I hadn't even known she'd re-joined the fight. One of her wings were torn and bloody and an arm had been broken. The arm that had been holding onto Carlos's soul.

"I'm sorry, when I saw them all attacking you, I-I just-"

I shook my head, silencing her. "Don't apologise. You did what you thought you had to do," I assured her.

"But I....lost the soul."

I shrugged. "It's okay, Reign. I'll just follow my bond with Aimee from here on out."

When she made to get up, I pushed her back down so that she was sitting again.

"Alone," I told her. "I'm going to follow the bond alone."

"But you need someone to have your back!" She protested loudly. "You can't take him on alone, Mary."

I smiled at her as I eased her wing into a different position so that it wasn't bent awkwardly. She hissed in pain before a sigh of relief followed.

"Thank you."

"I won't face him alone, Reign," I assured her. "I'm just following the bond to Aimee by myself. I'm relying on the others to join me in time to face him."

"I'll follow you soon, I swear," she promised me, gazing up at me pleadingly. "My wing will just take some time to heal but as soon as I'm done, I'll follow you."

I nodded and hugged her. I handed her one of my guns.

"Be careful," I murmured.

"No, *you* be careful. I'm safe here thanks to you. But *you're* the one walking into danger."

As I stood, she yanked on my hand, drawing my eyes back to her.

"Don't die."

I couldn't help the chuckle that bubbled up my throat.

"I'll do my best."

-X-

The trip there had taken longer than expected, but I couldn't help it when one of my legs failed on me several times. It seems I held Hysteria longer than I should have.

"Damn you," I cursed my right leg after the sixth time it gave out.

I turned my back to the wall I had been using to help keep moving and slid down until I was sitting on the concrete foot path.

Though I had taken in a lot of blood from my enemies, my body simply hadn't recovered from the immense strain I had put it under. Truthfully, it would take me a few days to be at my best again.

Having caught my breath and allowed my leg to rest for a moment, I was up again and moving.

Despite knowing I wasn't as strong as I could be, I kept moving. The wisp like touches at the back of my mind kept me motivated and determined to continue down the path.

"This smell..."

My feet stumbled to a stop, caught by surprise at the first cohesive thought since Aimee had woken up.

With my focus trained on the bond now, I was able to make out her feelings and thoughts through all the pain she was feeling.

"I know him."

Before I had time to realise it, my feet had started running. The sharp, burning pain in my leg seemed trivial now, compared to the task at hand.

I tried to mentally grasp the bond, as if it was somehow tangible.

"I'm coming, Aimee, I'm coming!"

But it wasn't enough. As Aimee fell unconscious due to the pain, our connection dropped. I could no longer find her.

I dropped to my knees as despair washed over me and the first wave of tears began to spill. She was lost to me.

"No," I whispered, my voice shaking. "No!" I screamed out, one of my hands clutching at my chest, my heart.

"Wake up!" I pleaded.

I folded into myself, my hands close to my chest as I seemed to curl into a ball, my head practically touching the ground, rocking.

She was so close! I knew she was close but-

A gentle breeze rustled my hair, but it wasn't the wind that caught my attention. It was scent that came with it.

Blood.

With nothing left to go on, nothing else to hope for, I followed that scent. My body was screaming at me but I wouldn't stop. I couldn't. My best friend needed me.

Hysteria of a different kind captured my heart and had me running through the bush towards the blood. Branches snapped and cracked as I forced my way passed them, unwilling to change my path for something as insignificant as a twig. My brash actions left me with many cuts but with all things considered, I couldn't find it within me to care at the moment.

My nose led me to an acreage though the air was polluted with the scent of blood. I was up the long driveway in an instant, dodging the expensive car. Considering how grand the house was and the jacked up car on the driveway, I guess it's safe to say the owners of the property were loaded with cash.

Cautiously, I limped into the house. The first room I passed by, I paused, taking in all the blood. At the centre of the room was a man, presumably the man of the house. Gently moving him, I noticed post mortem had set in. He'd been dead for at least four days. The next room was the kitchen and I picked up a different scent. A vampire.

As I got to the stairs, I found the body of a woman. My nose twitched. The woman was the vampire that I could smell in the kitchen. Looking at the winding staircase, there was a blood trail as if the woman had been dragged down them.

From what I could gather so far, the man was the first to be killed. He tried fending off his attacker while the woman ran for the stairs. That didn't make sense though. If the woman was a vampire, why didn't she fight the intruder instead?

Slowly, I headed up the stairs, unsure of what I'd find.

As I reached the top, my eyes landed on the dangling rope for the attic staircase. Looking down the hallway, I spotted a door slightly ajar. Moving towards it, I carefully peaked inside and suddenly understood.

Swiftly, I went back to the rope. Pulling it, I released the stairs. Once they had touched ground, I made my way up. I moved silently and listened for any hint of having company when it came as a soft gasp.

My eyes snapped over to the right, the darkest corner where a stack of boxes towered. Despite the lack of movement where even the dust particles seemed frozen in the air, I could hear quiet, rapid breathing.

I stepped sideways, little by little until the owner of the breathing came into view.

"Please don't hurt me!"

My heart fluttered as I stared at the tiny child before me. Her auburn hair clung to her sweaty forehead, slick thanks to the heat of the attic. From what I could see, she would be fair skinned, but she had a sickly complexion. Her face was hollow and her eyes glowed red.

Considering the scenario downstairs, I came to the conclusion that she was just like me; a dhampir. Though she was a small thing, she was still dangerous. Vampire children required a lot more blood then adult vamps. They didn't know how to control their hunger, their thirst. Her glowing eyes were a testament to her blood thirst. Just how long had she been hiding up here?

"It's okay," I soothed, slowly getting down to sit on the floor and appear less threatening. "What's your name?"

"Alia," she sniffed, though her eyes never moved from me.

"That's a beautiful name," I spoke, smiling at her. "My name is Mary. How old are you?"

She raised her shaking hands holding up seven fingers.

"You're seven? Wow, you're already a young lady," I cooed.

She blinked and lowered her hands. "R-Really? You really think so?"

I nodded enthusiastically. "Of course! Tell me, Alia, do you know what a vampire is?"

She nodded. "Mama is a vampire. She said I'm special because I'm half vampire and half human like papa."

"That's right. You're just like me. I'm half vampire, half human too!"

"Was your mama a vampire too?" She asked in awe.

"No, my papa was a vampire and my mama was a human."

"Whoa," she murmured.

"Do you drink blood, Alia?"

She shook her head. "No, mama used to mix the red stuff into my food. I don't know how to drink it properly yet."

"You must be thirsty."

She nodded, her eyes flashing at the reminder.

She raised to her feet and fumbled with one of the boxes she was hiding behind when she pulled out a blood pack. I looked inside the box to see it was filled with blood packs.

"Mama works as a nurse," she spoke proudly.

"That's handy," I muttered to myself before looking back at Alia.

Looking around, I spotted a baby's bottle. No doubt from Alias' newborn years. Grabbing one, I tried to clean it with some part of my shirt that wasn't already coated in blood.

"Alia, can you tell me what happened downstairs? How long have you been up here in the attic?"

She shuddered and seemed to fold into herself, trying to make herself smaller then she already was.

"It was raining when the monster came. I heard loud noises and yelling and I went out to see what it was. Mama ran upstairs and I saw-" she choked up, her bottom lip trembling as she sniffed.

I carefully opened up a blood pack, watching as her head snapped up to the smell. It was only then that I noticed I couldn't smell anything outside the attic. I bet it works vice versa. No wonder no one came looking for her up here. I steadily poured the blood into the bottle before screwing on the lid.

"Take your time, Alia. You're being very brave," I assured her as I offered the bottle.

She seemed hesitant to take it so I proved it was safe by drinking a little of it myself. It might be old but blood was blood. It wasn't as if she'd really notice the difference considering she wasn't old enough to compare it to anything.

The next time I offered the bottle to her, she took it before she suckled slowly, cautiously. Her crimson eyes widened and suddenly she couldn't drink the blood fast enough. I had another pack ready by the time she finished off the bottle.

When she held the bottle out to me, her newfound strength practically slammed it into me.

"More please!"

Despite everything, I couldn't help but chuckle. I took the bottle and refilled it. Between her sips, she continued her story.

"When I was at the top of the stairs, I saw the monster tearing up Papa. Mama ran to me and urged me inside the attic and told me to wait until someone got me."

When she had finished the bottle again, she didn't give it back to me. It lowered to her lap as her eyes dropped, suddenly saddened.

"Mama died, didn't she?"

I wanted more then anything to tell her that her loved ones were fine but I knew from personal experience that it would be better to tell her the truth now than to give her false hope.

"I heard her scream. The monsters killed her too."

"I'm sorry."

Honestly, what else was there to say?

"Wait...did you say monster*s*? There was more than one?"

She nodded. "I saw him join the monster before Mama made me come up here."

"Alia, do you know why they attacked your parents?"

She shook her head. "No, but they might have gone under the house."

"Under the house?" I wondered.

Alia nodded. "Mama often went down there. She kept a special mirror there. She said it let her visit her family."

Visit her family? Could it be a portal to Tavina?

"What did the beast look like, Alia?" I asked her.

"He was really big with grey fur. He looked like a large dog."

Carlos.

This has to be it. This *has* to be where Aimee is!

I stood, brushing of the dust I had collected from the floor.

"Please, don't leave me!" Alia exclaimed, suddenly clinging to my waist.

I looked down to stare at her terrified, blue eyes, the red having faded due to her thirst being quenched.

"Take me with you," she pleaded.

I placed my hand on her head, her dark locks silky to my callous touch.

"I can't right now. I'm going to find the bad men and I'll make them pay for what they did to your parents."

She blinked up at me. "You promise?"

I nodded and rustled her hair. "Yeah. I promise."

She let go and stepped back.

"Stay up here and don't make a sound. I'll come get you when I'm done, I promise."

She nodded and went straight back to her little hiding place. As I headed back to the stairs, I shot her one last look.

"Remember," I spoke and held a finger to my lips.

She nodded and copied me before I walked down the steps and raised the ladder, closing her off from the carnage below.

28

REVELATIONS

MOVING FURTHER THROUGH THE HOUSE, I found another door. As I approached it, I caught a slight shimmer. Looking closely, I finally noticed it had an almost transparent protective barrier around it. As I touched it, my hand was repelled, burning.

The pain though was familiar, something Amelia had taught to me about the different types of barriers and security measures vampires take. The spell was Regalia, only those of ancient blood could enter.

Swiping some of my blood from one of my many small wounds, I drew the ancient rune for Royalty, the barrier shimmering to my touch, glowing. Once completed, the bloody rune glowed brightly before it disappeared, the barrier along with it. I guess that's another good thing at being a dhampir; the only way you can be born is if one of your parents are of from the ancient families.

Without hesitation, I opened the door and my nose was assaulted by the strong scent of blood, but not just any blood; Aimees'.

"Guys, I think I found her," I warned the others.

Without waiting for a reply, I flew down the stairs without another thought, finding Aimee lying in the middle of the basement, on top of a large, bloody seal. She was alone. Though my soul screamed to take her away, my mind countered with knowledge of the ritual.

Once the glyph has been drawn in both the blood of the sacrifice and caster, very little can stop it now without the sacrifice dying.

Though this ritual is forbidden amongst the Draconis, they have come up with their own means to counter this dark spell. It requires blood of the caster as well as the combined blood of all three royal lines.

The blood must touch the sacrifice if keeping him/her alive is ones objective.

I could only stare at the bloodied body of my best friend, so close but still out of reach.

"Aimee," I called. "Aimee, I'm here. Look at me, please."

"I can't! Something's stopping me from moving!" She panicked. *"Do something, please!"*

From some of the ancient Latin writings used in the glyph, I could translate 'paralysis'. I translated more words that placed restriction on what Aimee could do. So far movement, speech and sight were taken away. But she could still hear me.

"I'm right here, Aimee," I soothed her. "The seal that's been drawn up has been activated. It's the reason you can't move, see or speak."

"But I could smell him!" She yelled, suddenly angry. *"Mary, it's-"*

"I'm surprised to see you here, my love."

Disbelief flooded my body like ice water. It couldn't be...

Slowly turning my head, I stared at the copper-haired vampire that I had come to love standing before a large full-body mirror, the surface rippling yet blank. It was the portal.

"Adam?" I breathed shakily.

He scoffed. "Don't give me that wounded look. You shouldn't be so surprised."

"Why are you doing this?" I asked, confused.

"For power, of course. Why else does anyone do anything?"

"Then you're...part of Vipera?"

He chuckled. "Part of it? My father is the king!"

My eyes widened. "You're the Prince?"

"Fitting that we should meet like this, isn't it?" He laughed.

When he saw my confused look, his mirth turned to disbelief.

"You're joking. You don't even know, do you?"

"Know what?" I wondered, tentatively.

"My father was the one who ordered the attack that killed yours."

I was silent as Adam moved, pacing the outline of the glyph, careful not to step inside. Instead of the lazy, casual walk I was used to, he held himself like all the other smug, noble vampires I'd come across.

"My father not only poisoned the blood your royal family drank, but he found your father and sent Vipera men after him."

The truth was suddenly crammed down my throat and difficult to swallow. "Your dad is the reason my parents are dead?"

Rage bubbled in my stomach, caressing my bloodlust and Adam's smug visage was doing little to quell it.

"But why?" The question spilled from my lips. "Why would he go to so much trouble to kill just one vampire?"

"Oh, honey," he mocked affectionately. "Your daddy wasn't just any vampire. He was a banished prince."

Prince? He couldn't mean-

"That's right, sweetheart," Adam spoke, though he spoke the term of endearment as if it sickened him. "Your daddy was from the main family. Amare is the purest line in the Draconis kingdom. Well, it *was*."

"But-...why? You said-"

"That I loved you?" He asked before he threw back his head and laughed. "Don't kid yourself, sweetheart. Not only are you from the Draconis kingdom," his laughter stopped but the vicious smirk never left his lips. "You're also a pathetic half-breed."

My stomach lurked but my anger sent me lunging for his throat.

"I trusted you!" I screamed, trying to get my hands on any part of him, though it was futile.

He kept dodging my attacks as if they were nothing.

"I expected more from an Amare," he spoke.

"How did you know?" I asked despite my rage and swiped again.

He dodged under and thrust a hard punch right into my stomach. I doubled over, wheezing before I felt him bring his elbow down on the back of my head. The force toppled me over, slamming me into the ground.

My body shook as I tried to move, to raise up onto my arms at least.

"I saw your rings."

My eyes darted over to my scarred arm, where the rings hid underneath the enchanted glove.

Of course. The rings that belonged to my father that Amelia said only he or his family could wear.

"Why do you think that giant lizard practically heeds your every beck and call?"

"Giant lizard?" I panted as I managed to get to my hands and knees. "You mean Jarrod? He has nothing to-"

I looked up at Adam who standing before the mirror again.

"On the contrary, there were so many signs that you clearly missed, Mary," he laughed, deciding to indulge in my ignorance. "Dragons by nature keep to themselves. No one is worthy of their time or attention. They're quite arrogant really. But when it comes to the Amare, they practically get down on their knees. The Basilisks are the same for the Ura, my family."

Appearing before me, he delivered a swift kick to my unprotected side and I flew into the stone wall, cracking it upon impact. I dropped to the ground, struggling to get up again. Then things took a turn for the worst.

"It's about time you showed up."

Looking up, I spotted the grey wolf that was supposed to be locked up in silver chains in my dungeon.

Instead of speaking, the beast snarled and picked me up by my hair.

"Back up would be great right now!"

I felt tickling at the back of my mind, knowing someone was looking through my eyes. I didn't need to guess because a second later, Cassidy and Reign appeared in a flash, one by me and Carlos and the other behind Adam.

Cassidy drove a silver dagger into Carlos's right shoulder blade, the pain causing him to loosen his grip and I dropped to the ground. I watched Reign's arms grab Adam in a headlock before she disappeared the same way she came. Cassidy grabbed my wrist and barely touched Carlos before we followed Reign and winked out of the basement and into the front yard where an ambush had been set, just as Reign was tossed away from Adam like a sack of potatoes.

Tori caught her as Chelsea shot forth and engaged him in combat, Tori joining her once Reign was safely on her feet again. Sensing someone coming, Cassidy grabbed me and took to the sky. From there, I watched as the Wolf Boys took our place and led Carlos further from Adam so that two different fights took place.

There was a sound behind us, causing me to look over my shoulder. I was wrong. Three battles took place. William and the others were holding off a horde of Vipera vampires. When it seemed like they were being overwhelmed, I spotted something far off in the distance. It grew closer by the second and by the time I recognised the silhouette as a full blown dragon, it unleashed a powerful blast of fire, engulfing everything in its path. The control over it's own power staggered me as the flames seemed to die before reaching my friends.

The dragon circled Cassidy and I as we hovered in the air before the massive creature paused so that it's face was right in front of me, eyes glaring into mine. It's large wings giving strong, steady waves as it kept level with me. It's large jaw opened just enough to huff out a breath of steam.

"Scared?"

"Jarrod!?" I gasped.

The dragon gave another huff that sounded more like a chuckle.

"You should see your face."

The amusement in his voice was undeniable.

"You're so...."

"Amazing? Awe inspiring? Terrifying?"

"Big."

"You need to expand your vocabulary."

I hugged the giant nose before me, relieved.

"Thank you for coming," I murmured.

"Anytime."

"Hold off the horde," I told him. "I've got an ex-fiancé to deal with."

He grunted his acknowledgement before he uncurled from around us and headed back to the Vipera vampires. I made gestures to William when he finally caught sight of me. The nod of his head told me he understood.

"Tori. Chels. Fall back."

Those two pulled away from Adam just as William, Rolan and Alistair took their place. Tori ran to help Mikai, Aura and Tiny finish off the vampires that Jarrod missed but Chelsea paused below us.

"He's too strong," she explained. *"I feel that the only way we could really make any ground is if we take out the wolf. Quickly."*

I nodded and she ran off to join Tori. I looked over at the wolves to see that though they had Carlos outnumbered, he had them outclassed. Their power dwarfed in comparison and that power was shared with Adam.

"Let me down by Carlos," I told Cassidy who did so without hesitation.

She swooped down and released me. I barrelled straight down, slamming into Carlos's back. He staggered forwards, but did not drop as I had hoped he would. Instead, Blade in his wolf form, barged into the back of his legs. This time, the larger beast couldn't stay upright and fell to his hands and knees.

This seemed to be the wrong thing because he disappeared from my sight, his speed having increased with the use of four powerful limbs instead of two. A cry of pain brought my attention to Leo who was sent flying back into the blue Lamborghini.

"What a waste," Tori called out from her position.

"Not the time!" Chelsea responded from beside her.

Jye soon followed, hitting the fence of the tennis court. Like Adam, Carlos was a freak of nature that needed to be put down. ASAP. But despite knowing this, no one could seem to land a blow on him and even between the five of us, we were struggling. As I felt the familiar panic in my heart, before I used Hysteria again to give me an edge against this monster, Chase arrived.

And he brought reinforcements.

Beside him stood his pack, the same pack that alienated Aimee only to accept her as Alpha. With him was Cameron, Cody and Mira, who hadn't died like I though from what Chase told me. With this new force, Carlos went down slowly but surely until Mira held him down with her jaws around his throat.

"Don't just kill him!" I heard Reign shout before she swooped over and landing before him.

"What the fuck do you mean?" Chase snapped. "This man-"

"No," she corrected herself. "I mean we need to cripple him first. If we cause him enough pain, it should go through the bond."

She turned to me.

"Right?"

I nodded. "So what's the plan?"

"I read the book you had on the ritual and I think Cass and I could reverse the effects."

"Do it," I agreed.

Mira looked wary of the new plan but her jaws didn't move from around his throat. Purple sparks drew my attention to Reign, her hand being the cause. Hovering by Carlos, she stared down at the wolf in concentration. Her hand gingerly touched his exposed chest before familiar purple electricity lit up the yard. Carlos screamed in agony and thrashed about but Miras' hold on his throat -as well as the wolf boys holding down his limbs- kept him from harming the angel.

With one final pull, his soul was back within her hands. Reign was panting, but a wicked smile graced her lips. Knowing what she wanted to do and what to look for, it took a lot less time for her to find the tie between the two souls.

Clenching the soul, Carlos screamed and continued resisting. I caught sight of Adam's slight falter and knew her plan was working.

"Keep going but when I say, you kill him."

Reign nodded and I left Carlos to her. When I turned away, my eyes instantly sought out Adam. He would pay for using me.

As I jumped back into the fight, I threw myself at him when he was focused on slamming William into the ground.

"I still don't understand how you found us," he spoke before one of my fist caught his jaw.

He jumped away, panting and tried to get his bearings but I followed after him, keeping up the pressure. I may not be as strong or fast, but I'm bloody persistent. Most of my attacks he blocked, but those openings he left were exploited to their fullest potential.

"Aimee and I are bound, the same as you and Carlos."

The information caught him by surprise, as did my kick to his groin. He wheezed and doubled over in pain.

"That's for fucking me over."

"You *bitch*," he hissed between clenched teeth and then before me, he seemed to radiate light like my scarlet Hysteria, only he was giving off of golden light.

"You're not the only one who can power up."

Then he was beating down on everyone. I found myself flat on my back but quickly rolled back to dodge Adam's following kick. Once upright, I called to Reign.

"Now!"

Reign found the Bond on Carlos' soul and severed it, cutting off their connection. Adam's pain-filled cries echoed Carlos' before Rolan and I kicked in the back of his knees while he was distracted, bringing him down.

"You fucking Amare!" He cursed at me. "You can never do anything alone! Your whole family is weak! You-"

Any other insults he may have had were cut off, just like his head. I could hear that Carlos had been silenced as well.

What vampires were left from the horde fled the moment they saw their prince fall. Without Adam to lead them, they could see they were clearly outmatched. As I stared down at the head of my fiancé in my hands, I couldn't help the tears that cried for the love we lost for though it was all a ruse for him, it had been real for me.

"Are you alright, Princess?"

I turned to William but took in the sight of five bowing vampires. William, Rolan, Mikai, Aura and Alistair were kneeling with their heads bowed and a fist over their heart with their palms pointed upwards. It hadn't been William that addressed me, it was Alistair.

"I need a Leal and Tare," I answered before heading back into the mansion.

I didn't question Jarrod as he followed closely. Turning, I saw it was William and Alistair that had come at my request. Before heading down to Aimee, I went back to the attic. I poked my head up while the boys stayed silent at the bottom of the ladder.

"Alia," I called softly.

From behind the box, I saw her auburn head poke out. Her eyes lit up when she saw me.

"It's safe to come out now."

She got up, spilling many empty blood packs onto the ground as she ran to my outstretched arm. Carefully, I swooped her up after shifting the decapitated head to my left arm and turned around to slowly climb back down, but had to pause because the three men were crowding the area.

"Can you guys just give me space?" I stressed.

They quickly backed up and I touched ground with Alia on one arm. Letting her down, she held onto my black jeans before I led them to Aimee. After giving them directions, Alistair and William flicked their blood onto Aimee's motionless body. The seal began to glow before I held Adam's head over it and let his blood join the mixture. Then for the last of the reversal, I dabbed my hand onto the gaping wound on my leg I obtained during the fight and splattered it all over the seal and Aimee. My blood caused the rune to glow purple before finally, the seal and all the blood vanished to nothing. Aimee's eyes shot open as she bolted upright.

Throwing Adam's head away, I was grasping at Aimee, pulling her close and rocking her gently, hushing her gasps and whimpers. I had her back. She was safe again. But as I looked over her shoulder at the True Borns and the dragon, I couldn't help but feel like there was so much more to come.

And it would make for one hell of a story.